# HOLISTIC HEAT

## ELEMENTS OF DANGER, BOOK 2

### WILLA BROOKS

WILLABROOK PUBLISHING INC.

WillaBrook Publishing Inc.

www.willabrooks.com

Cover by Willa Brooks

ISBN: 978-1-7778432-3-6

*For Ms. Rain, my first grade assistant teacher, who told me that my name appeared in lots of romance novels.*

# CONTENTS


Chapter 1     1
*Charlie*

Chapter 2     10
*Carol Lynne*

Chapter 3     21

Chapter 4     26

Chapter 5     37
*Charlie*

Chapter 6     44

Chapter 7     51
*Carol Lynne*

Chapter 8     56

Chapter 9     59
*Charlie*

Chapter 10     62
*Carol Lynne*

Chapter 11     68

Chapter 12     78
*Charlie*

Chapter 13     84
*Carol Lynne*

Chapter 14     92
*Charlie*

Chapter 15     97

Chapter 16     103
*Carol Lynne*

Chapter 17     112

Chapter 18     119

Chapter 19     134

Chapter 20     146

Chapter 21 — 157
*Charlie*

Chapter 22 — 168
*Carol Lynne*

Chapter 23 — 176

Chapter 24 — 185
*Charlie*

Chapter 25 — 193
*Carol Lynne*

Chapter 26 — 201
*Charlie*

Chapter 27 — 210
*Carol Lynne*

Chapter 28 — 213

Chapter 29 — 218

Chapter 30 — 227

Chapter 31 — 232

Chapter 32 — 238
*Charlie*

Chapter 33 — 241
*Carol Lynne*

Chapter 34 — 246

Chapter 35 — 252

Chapter 36 — 258

Chapter 37 — 267

Chapter 38 — 272

Chapter 39 — 283

Chapter 40 — 288

Chapter 41 — 295
*Charlie*

Chapter 42 — 300
*Carol Lynne*

Chapter 43 — 303

Epilogue                                        308
Timberwolf                                      315

*(excerpt from Timberwolf, Chapter I*

*Afterword*                                     329
*Also by Willa Brooks*                          331

# CHAPTER 1
### CHARLIE

The clock display on my desk read 4:45 p.m. Perfect. The lawyers were about to leave for the weekend. I grabbed my phone, unlocked it and scrolled through my contacts. Then I sent a text to the only woman who could help me.

**Charlie Stevenson:** Overtime?
**Amberly Davidson:** Ok :)

I smiled, turned off my phone, and tried to focus on a legal pad filled with facts for this confusing case. But I couldn't wrap my head around it because it swam as it usually did at the end of the workweek.

After Amberly and I worked *overtime*, my mind will be clear enough to get some work done.

I twirled the pen through my fingers while staring down at my scribbling on the legal pad. But nothing came. This damned case was air-tight.

The black, leather office chair creaked when I got up, walked over to the window, and stared out at the glass building across the street.

It was close enough to see what happened inside. I found it entertaining and enlightening to watch people in their natural habitat when they didn't realize it.

Thank God for fluorescent lighting.

A gentle knock on the door interrupted my thoughts.

"Come in," I said with a wide grin.

Amberly Davidson, our receptionist, timidly came in, closed the door, and turned the lock on the doorknob.

It surprised me that she was still shy. Most women in her position would have been sure of themselves by now, but not her.

The buxom redhead walked in wearing a black shirt that molded to her mouth-watering tits. Her red skirt showcased her rounded ass, and I would bet my life that she wore a thong.

No panty lines.

Her black bag hung on her shoulder. She wore a cute, messy ponytail that she reached behind her head and pulled out the elastic. Then, she put both hands in her hair and shook it. The action caused her massive tits to bounce.

*Nice.*

She walked into my office bathroom and shut the door.

I headed over to my desk, opened the locked bottom drawer with my key, and wrestled a condom out from the box I hid under a stack of reference books.

Tossing it across the room, it landed on the couch by the window. I'd always handled condoms.

One of Dad's pearls of wisdom he passed as soon as I started dating.

Never trusted women enough not to poke a hole in them.

In fact, he said it so much that I wondered if that was how my mother became pregnant with me. Maybe that was why Dad felt obligated to marry her. I wouldn't put condom tampering past her because that woman was a Class A gold digger.

Not that I could see Amberly doing anything like that, but still, when so much money was at play, you couldn't tell.

Even though Amberly was sweet and would make a great mom someday, I don't want that kind of commitment. So I'd casually suggested she go on birth control pills.

Unbuttoning my white shirt, I took it off, and carefully set it on the back of my chair so that it wouldn't crease, then did the same with my tanned pants. With lightning speed, I stripped out of the rest of my clothes.

Amberly opened the bathroom door. She wore the lilac, silk one-piece lingerie I bought her.

Her plump, round tits pushed the fabric to its limits. Amberly's nipples were taut and looked as though they would pierce the silk.  Her deep-red, shoulder-length hair cascaded around her shoulders.

She sashayed to the couch. I glued my eyes to her big beautiful ass as she moved. She knelt on the sofa and leaned over the back, staring out the window as she'd done every time we were together.

It struck what it meant that she wore lingerie. She had been expecting this.

I frowned. Shit, I was becoming predictable.

Shoving that thought out of my head, I walked up behind her and pressed my body against her back.

"Care to play?" I whispered in her ear, starting our role-play.

"Yes, boss." Her voice, breathy.

"Been thinking about me all day, haven't you?" My dick hardened as I ground it along her ass crack.

"Yes, boss," she replied.

I pulled away from her and ran my hands up and down her smooth ass, then slapped one cheek, then the other. Running my fingers between her legs, I cupped her pussy and massaged her clit through the fabric. She threw her head back and moaned.

"Shh," I whispered in her ear.

I removed my fingers and ran both hands up her arms to the shoulder straps. Then I moved them off, peeled the fabric away from her tits, and filled my hands with them. Their heaviness made me gasp and ground deeper into her ass crack.

The redhead moaned and gyrated on my cock. Her day-old perfume's light floral scent filled my nose.

One of my hands covered her breasts while the other trailed down her torso, then lower to play with her clit through the silk fabric.

Her ass rubbed against my cock like she was begging for more.

I whispered in her ear, "You ready for me, sweetheart?"

Amberly nodded and continued to grind.

I whispered, "You promise to fuck me real good?"

She nodded again.

"Are you gonna feed me these jugs while bouncing up and down on my cock?"

Amberly moaned that time.

Satisfied I'd gotten her wet enough to slide in quickly, I grabbed the condom and ripped open the wrapper. Taking out the rubber, I fitted it on the tip of my dick and rolled it down.

Sitting down on the black leather couch, the material squeaked under my weight.

Amberly threw a leg over my lap, straddling me.

I moved the crotch of the panties to the side and positioned my dick at her entrance.

Amberly grabbed my shoulders and slid down easily. We gasped.

She moved up and down slowly while I fastened my eyes on her tits. As she picked up speed, her tits bounced.

Unable to hold myself back, I took one into my mouth, sucking and flicking her nipple with my tongue. Then I moved to the other side to give it attention.

Amberly moved harder, and I swallowed a growl as the ache in my groin intensified.

I squeezed her ass cheeks and powered up, so my tip tapped the back of her.

Amberly's fingers nails dug into my shoulders. Their bite fueled me on. She gasped with each thrust.

I moved harder and faster.

Her tightness made my eyes roll back.

My. Fucking. God!

Amberly matched my speed, and her pussy clenched around my shaft. It took a gargantuan effort not to lose it right there. My body and mind fought against the impending rush. My balls tightened in response.

I moved faster while she tensed. Her body seized while her pussy pulsated.

I drove for a few more strokes until I let go, allowing the storm to rage. My feral growl caught in my throat.

We stilled, catching our breaths.

Amberly kissed my neck then got up. She went to the bathroom and locked the door. Muffled sounds of the zipper, the crinkling of plastic, and the tap from the sink, came from inside.

Rushing back to my desk, I grabbed a few tissues, took the condom off, then tossed it in the trash. Pulling open the bottom drawer, I grabbed the bottle of hand sanitizer and squirted some in my palm, and rubbed my hands.

I snatched hand wipes and ran them along my body, trying to remove the scent of Amberly.

Then I dressed as quickly as possible while making sure my clothes looked unruffled.

Glancing over the notes, one fact caught my attention when Amberly opened the bathroom door.

"Bye Charlie, have a good weekend."

Preoccupied, I answered, "See ya."

She hesitated by the door before she quietly slipped out.

Five minutes later, someone knocked.

Dad came in without being invited and stood by the entrance with his hand on the knob. He wore his usual white button-down shirt with red suspenders attached to his black pants. His curly, dark brown hair sat like a heap on his head while the sides were trimmed close. He resembled that nerdy singer from the '50s. Maybe it was his black-framed glasses that stamped it.

Way different from my brown hair and muscular build. Bri and I had the same hair color and took after our mother in that respect. Though I wish I were taller like my father.

"Any luck yet?" He referred to the case I was working on.

"No, not yet. I think we may have to find a way to settle. They won't be able to get around the new privacy laws. Up until now, the data brokers had a free for all." I answered my dad.

He raised his eyebrows. With his hands in his pockets, he stood on the balls of his feet when he got excited. "Those laws aren't retroactive. The key to winning this case is time. Find out when the info was sold. If it falls within the ninety-day window of when the law was passed, we still have a case."

I nodded at him, "Thanks, Dad." My tone was calm despite my clenched fists. I wanted to punch a hole through the fucking wall. Of course, I should have looked at the time window. What the fuck was I thinking?

He smiled at me and said, "Have a nice weekend," and closed the door.

I leaned back in my chair, looked up at the ceiling, and squeezed my eyes shut. My fists were pressed to my forehead. I hated looking like I just graduated from law school in front of him. I fucking *hated* it.

# CHAPTER 2
## CAROL LYNNE

The first thing I did when I got home from work—or as people on the commune called it, "the rat race," was take off my gold chain link necklace, bracelet, and earrings.

The thump of the jewelry box slamming shut gave a strong sense of satisfaction because they were more like dog tags than decorative. Sometimes, I wore my Buddha beads but not this evening because my neck was already damp with sweat.

The red cotton briefs and a white cami would suffice since it was rare that people came over.

Since my best friend, Sarah, came by less frequently —well, rarely, I'd taken a shine to being half-naked. People thought because I'd grown up in a commune, or as we called it, an intentional community, I'd be okay with being naked. But it wasn't anything like that. Besides, who in their right mind did farm work naked?

Pulling out the elastic that held my blonde hair in a clean ponytail, I flipped it over, gathered it, and retied it into a messy top bun.

Not wanting to cook after my shitty day, I opened my freezer door to make a selection from the variety of frozen organic meals. My kitchenette comprised of a small fridge, a stove, and a sink that occupied the space of the back wall. It looked like it was part of the living room.

The phone binged with a notification of an incoming text. I closed the freezer and went to the table beside my patchwork couch to see who it was.

**Charlie High Falutin' Stevenson:** Can I come over? I'm feeling sort of down.

**Carol Lynne Miller:** No. Sorry, My day was fucked up. And I don't feel like having company right now.

There was a knock on my door. I rolled my eyes. Sheesh, this man took liberties whenever he wanted. There went arrogance for ya.

"Hold your horses!" I shouted at the door, then ran into my bedroom, grabbed a pair of tanned shorts from my dresser drawer, and slid it on.

I hurried out of the room, buttoning and zipping up my shorts along the way. After turning the locks, I pulled open the door to a hulking Charlie.

He stood there in brown aviator glasses, a white shirt, and tanned slacks. His hair was shorter since the last time he was here, but his beard was still scruffy.

My heart fluttered, and I promptly squashed it. Having feelings for this man was dangerous. Sure, we slept together a few times. My reactions towards him were nothing more than a memory of a great orgasm. It wasn't like I was looking for a commitment, nor would he offer one.

"Come in and tell me about your shitty day, but you'll have to hear about mine. You're warned," I narrowed my eyes.

Charlie walked in with a faint smile on his square face. That jaw made him look like a sexy Neanderthal.

"You didn't have to rush to get dressed. I've seen you naked, remember?"

Oh, I remember. Trust me. And I tried to forget it but can't. But I won't caress the ego of this arrogant prick, so I rolled my eyes, deliberately dismissing his question. After we had sex the first time, he was weird afterward—typing on his phone and writing notes in his book. Not gonna lie, it hurt my feelings, so I kicked him out of my apartment.

When he talked me into it the second time, I knew what to expect and told him that he had to leave immediately after. He was too good to refuse, and as much as it pained to admit, I needed physical contact. Needless to say, he was shocked, and frankly, I was surprised he accepted my terms. That was the second time we hooked up.

I was holding out for Mr. Right, but at this rate, I seriously doubted he existed. Perhaps all we could hope for was Mr. Right now. *Charlie.*

As he walked by, there was a red stain on his neck.

"Are you bleeding?" I called out and turned his collar down for a closer inspection.

Charlie's expression morphed from curious to sheepish. "Naw, that was from my girl."

*His girl?* Since when did he have a girl?

I froze, the fire of humiliation engulfed my body. I cleared my throat, readjusted his collar, and said, "Sorry. I should've minded my own business." I scooted away and led him to the patchwork couch, feeling like I'd been slapped.

While we settled, I hugged my red mandala toss pillow and tried to breathe past the pain in my tight throat. If he aired what was on his mind, he could leave, and I'd finally put this shitty day to rest.

"So, what's up?" I prompted, wanting him to get this over with.

"I had a case that I couldn't find a way around except to offer a settlement. Dad figured out a loophole in like two seconds. I'm paranoid that he'll look down on me, and I may lose my good standing as someone he'll pass the company to."

"You think he'd look down on you because he offered you a suggestion? If that's all it takes to look down on a person, then—"

"Look, he's a good man, but he wants me to earn the company," Charlie cut in.

"And you think you're less deserving if he figures out something faster than you? Ray has had years of experience. I'm sure his mind is trained to pick up details that you'd miss. And so what if you're not the best lawyer, at least you're hard-working, and that counts for something, right? You can prove your worth in other ways."

He raised a heavy brow, "How?"

"Well, even if you don't win all your cases, you can still do things on the business end to make sure your dad's firm is perceived as one of the finest in the country. Find ways to drum up more business."

Charlie stared at his clasped hands, lost in thought. I just sat and watched our reflection on the blank TV screen. My throat chakra was blocked, probably because I'd been fighting a scream since I got home.

"So tell me why your day was so shitty." He interrupted my thoughts.

I blew out a breath. "I got fired today."

He reared back. Something about his reaction made me hike one side of my lips. I'd blame it on the fact that his privileged ass figured out that there were other people with problems a little more significant than looking like a simpleton in front of your daddy. Some people didn't even know their daddy.

"What? How? You seem like the type to be diligent at work." He sounded confused.

*Type.* A classification. My spirits fell further, and I deadpanned, "I didn't fuck anything up. I got fired because the lady who was my competition for the job got promoted. And since we never got along—" I shrugged.

"Is there any recourse you can take, I mean legally?"

I gaped at him. Was he offering me help? "No. They're mailing my severance pay since I have a contract."

He squinted and slightly shook his head. "Why are

you so calm? Shouldn't you be in tears?"

I pursed my lips. "Saw it comin'. That was why I started this new gig in the first place. Looks like I'm going to be a concert promoter full-time. Eventually, I'd like to turn it into a charity leg of concert tours where bands can donate their earnings for that concert to charity.

But first, I need to build up my reputation, so I'm working on putting together regularly scheduled shows. I have a gig tomorrow night, so I don't have time to be upset."

"Sounds cool. You told me about the concert when I drove you home from the hospital. Neat idea about the charity leg too. Hope it works out." he said, then glanced at his Rolex and stood up. "I gotta get going."

Not exactly. We talked about the concert I threw last summer, not the one tomorrow night. *Nice* to see he paid attention.

Thank goodness he was leaving. I stood up. "Thanks for dropping by." Not really, but Momma raised me to have manners even when I didn't feel like it.

"Thanks for talking to me, and I'm sorry about your job, Sugar."

*Ugh.* Sugar. He called me that after he found out I was from Mississippi. I told him to stop, but as I'd discovered, if you tell him to do anything, it'll only encourage him to do it more. I bet he kept his beard out of spite because his dad was on his case about shaving.

I led him to my front door and opened it. We said our goodbyes, and I closed it. Relief, relaxed my tight chest. Finally! I could let loose and cry without shame. I slipped off my shorts and returned them to the drawer when my phone rang. Oh, fuck my life!

I hurried back to the living room.  After taking a gander at the long numbers on the screen, I guessed who it was. A pang of regret hit my heart as I swiped the green button.

"Hey, Momma. How're ya doing?" There was a pause before she responded in her southern accent. Her voice was deep and slightly raspy.

"Carol Lynne? You on your smartphone?"

"Yes, Momma. Is everything okay? You're calling from the payphone at the convenience store down yonder, aren't ya?"

"Oh, yeah, everything is okay over here, Sweet Pea. How about you?" Her tone was filled with concern. Dang, she can already tell. I must sound like shit.

"Well, I got fired today." No need to beat around the bush, I guess.

"Does that mean you're comin' home?" The hope

that filled her voice made my heart ache. She was lonely. That was what happened when you're the social pariah on a commune. She and my biological father ran away to that community. The founder fell in love with my dad. Guess who won that battle for that loser's heart? *Free love? Nothin' was ever free.*

"No, Momma, it doesn't. I had a feeling this would've happened, so I started another business as a concert promoter, and I'm working tomorrow night. As much as this sucked, it wasn't the worst thing that could've happened."

That reminded me that Keith's band was playing at the concert. I didn't trust he'd remember to attend the sound check because his drunkenness was a common state.

She laughed good-naturedly, snapping me back to attention. "That's my Sweet Pea. Like a cat, always landin' on yer feet."

"Yes, Ma'am. I'll be fine. But how are you?"

She sighed, "Plumb tuckered. Business is boomin' at the restaurant, so my toes are hollerin' at the end of the day."

Yeah, I know. All that manual labor with nothing to show for it. My mother was a cook in the restaurant on River Run Farms and works for one hundred dollars per month. I'd tried to send her money over the years, so she didn't need to spend hers, but she told me that she didn't need much to get by. I told her that it wasn't about getting by, it was about leverage.

She said she didn't need it or anything else. The only time she did was when she called and begged for seven hundred dollars for a new mattress.

She hesitated. "Just callin' to check up on ya. It's been a while since we talked or even saw each other."

"I know, Momma. I might have more time now that I'm running my own business. Maybe I can come to visit for a while."

"That would be wonderful, Sweet Pea. I'd look forward to that." The excitement in her voice tweaked my heart. I'd been such a bad daughter.

"Or, I could send you some money, so you can buy a plane ticket to visit me."

"Oh darlin', you're sweeter than sugar, but I can't get away. You're gonna have to come down here."

I frowned, "Okay, I'll do that. Love you, Momma."

She hesitated for a beat, like there was something she was about to say. "Love you too. Bye, Sweet Pea."

"Bye, Momma."

That was weird. Something nagged me but I couldn't put my finger on it. Sucks because I would've helped her in any way I could if she asked.

I took a bag of frozen leftover vegan chili out of the freezer and popped it in the microwave. Then I turned on my laptop while waiting for my food to heat up.

The footsteps of my neighbor echoed in the hall outside. His keys jingled as he turned the lock. I got up, ran to my door, and opened it quickly before he disappeared.

I called out, "Keith, wait!" The tall, skinny, dark-haired man jerked in surprise. His eyes stayed wide open as they traveled down my body. My eyes followed his and looked down at my bare legs.

"Fuck!" I shouted, scrambled back into my apartment, and slammed the door.

# CHAPTER 3

The following morning, I stood up from my seat while the train pulled into the station on Fourteenth Street. The rumble under my feet caused me to shuffle to the doors waiting for it to come to a stop.

After the doors parted, I stepped off and climbed up the stairs with a handful of people. I pushed through the turnstile and climbed up another flight of stairs to the street.

The warm, muggy summer air hit like a wall, causing sweat to run down my forehead. After walking up the block, a beautiful brown awning with a classy white font which read *Glow,* appeared like a beacon. Boho clothing displayed on hangers hung from the awning supports which was customary in downtown Manhattan.

A clothing rack, a table with crates of books, and toss pillows were on display outside the store. Why they weren't afraid that people would steal anything was beyond me. We didn't have that kind of setup back in Mississippi, that was for sure.

A little bell rang, as I pushed the door open. Asian lanterns in vibrant yellows, pinks, and emerald-green colors hung from the ceiling. An array of wind chimes of different metals shimmered beside them. An assortment of charts were mounted to the wall. A stand packed with packages of incense gave the store an exotic scent. Clothing racks and jewelry stands were scattered like a maze.

The oddest thing of all was a disco ball that hung from the middle of the ceiling. But who was I to judge?

I waved at Cheryl, the owner who had short, curly platinum-blond hair and big red glasses.

She wiped down the counter that she stood behind and said, "Nice to see you, Carolyn. It's been a while. Thought you moved away."

I didn't even correct her for messing up my name and called out over my shoulder, "Nah, still here. Just busy with workin' two jobs."

I stopped by the incense stand to make my selection.

She grinned, "I hear ya."

I smiled back at her and returned my attention to the stand. There was a vast selection, but I zeroed in on a resealable plastic bag filled with wooden sticks of Palo Santo. The neon green sticker indicated that it was on sale for fifteen dollars.

A box filled with six bundles of smudging sage cost twenty dollars. I picked them up, made my way to Cheryl, and placed the packages on the checkout counter because this store didn't offer shopping baskets.

She set them aside to make room for the rest of my inevitable purchases.

I stopped at a cute wind chime in the sun's shape with an orange center that had little bells hanging from its squiggly rays. It could liven my dull living room, or so I hoped.

My hand shot up as I pointed to the chime and said, "Cheryl, I'd like that orange wind chime." She walked out from behind the counter wearing a black t-shirt and a mid-knee-length skirt. She grabbed the reach pole that rested against the wall and unhooked the chime, then took it to the counter with the rest of my stuff.

A beautiful oval-shaped pendant that hung from the jewelry stand, caught my eye. It looked like it contained lava and was fastened to a simple black corded necklace. It would be a perfect addition to the outfit I planned on wearing to the concert tonight.

After running a few more errands which included a stop at the Showtime Deli for meal purchases, I walked up the stairs to my apartment with shopping bags a half-hour later.

When I got to the landing, Keith was about to open the door to his apartment.

He smirked when our eyes met. "Glad you remembered to wear clothes before going out, this time."

I rolled my eyes. "You've seen less on a woman. What I did shouldn't have been so scandalous."

His face turned sheepish, and he went inside. Hah. *Bitch*. That'll teach him to goad me. Some people can't help being dicks. But dang, I didn't talk to him about the concert. Oh well, if he doesn't show up, I know where he lives.

I went inside and turned on the little black Bluetooth speaker that sat by the TV, and opened the music app on the laptop. The comforting strains of Bob Dylan's *Like a Rolling Stone* filled the room while I ate lunch.

I scanned through emails. No issues with the bands

or, God forbid, any change in plans tonight. After everything was squared away, I dug out the package of Palo Santo from the bag, a midnight blue ceramic dish and lighter from the TV stand's cabinet, and lit the wood stick on fire.

The woodsy scent filled the air. It took me back to singing around the campfire when I was a little girl. The hiss and crackle of burning twigs joined our voices while lightning bugs provided points of light.

I shoved that memory aside and held up the wind chime to decide where it would sparkle the best. The light that came in from the window would make it sparkle, and would remind me that the sun was out, even in this shitty apartment.

Hunting through the coat closet, I took a small hook from the stash in my toolbox. Then I stacked a pile of meditation pillows on a chair, climbed it, and tried not to fall while screwing the hook into the ceiling.

Slipping the string of the chime on the hook, I hopped down, and admired its shimmer. Hoping it possessed some kind of curative power to lift this dreadful funk, I waited. And waited. Then the hope faded, taking my mood with it.

A few hours later, I changed into black jeans, a white t-shirt, and a black blazer. I donned my new fire pendant. Then, I packed my sandwich and a few

# CHAPTER 4

The production crew, attired in black, swarmed as the hum of their chatter magnified in the auditorium. Some were on stage, adjusting the mic stands, while others laid cables and tested the lights.

Standing at the bottom of the stage, a man spoke into a walkie-talkie while he watched the control room at the back.

Through all of this, a familiar man who looked like Little Orphan Annie and Opie's son, rushed up to me while I clipped a pass to the lapel of my jacket.

His headset with a mouthpiece attachment was swallowed by his curly orange 'fro. He wore black jeans and a faded, black polo shirt. That was Ben Finley, the runner.

"Hey, Carolyn. The water delivery still isn't here," his eyes were saucered and his forehead puckered.

"What's the holdup?" I asked, already crossing my eyes.

"They turned up at the wrong place, so they'll be a little late. The driver called and said they're in transit and were on their way."

I drew in breath to quell the sudden spike in my heart rate and asked, "Do you have a contingency plan if they don't make it?"

"No, Ma'am." He contemplated his feet and squinted for a second. "I'll run to the store and buy some, but we don't need to do that just yet because the delivery guy said he'll be here."

I gulped. Dang. Maybe I should stockpile water cases, so I didn't need to rely on a secondary company last minute. But where would I keep them? There wasn't tons of space in my hovel.

I entered it into the to-do list of things to research on my phone.

While erasing mistakes my fingers made by hitting the wrong keys, Ben said, "If we're cool, I'll get back to work."

"Sure. Let me know if anything else comes up." I mumbled, distracted.

He hurried off.

I climbed the steps that led to the stage. The wide space below filled with the crew will be replaced by cheering fans in a few hours. If this concert goes down as I'd planned, this will be my second successful event in a year.

The last time I produced a show, I worked a full-time job, and the hours nearly killed me. Ben would text about problems that needed looking into.

After work, I lugged my tired fanny to the venue and dealt with them until the wee hours in the morning, got up early the next day for my job, and did it all over again.

I should send Jackie Levin some roses to thank her because it would only piss her off. Then again, that was probably not the best course of action.

No point in wasting beautiful flowers on a witch. Better to just soldier on. Besides, I would've wanted to keep them.

I tapped an order on my phone to be delivered to my apartment as a congratulatory gift for putting on this gig as I meandered backstage.

A side door opened, and a brown-uniformed delivery guy backed into the hallway while wheeling a dolly with cases of bottled water down the hall to the back.

I expelled a breath. Never doubt Ben.

The stage manager, Maurice Davenport, came up to me. He was a stocky man with brown combed back hair, glasses, and wore a black button-down shirt and blue jeans. "Carolyn, there you are. Hope I'd catch you before the show."

I cringed internally but didn't correct him. "Sure, Maurice. What's on your mind?"

"How many people are going to be here? That includes the concert-goers as well as acts, so we don't exceed the fire code."

I flashed a smile, "Let me take a gander, and I'll get back to you right quick."

He nodded, thanked me, and dashed off.

As I scrolled down the spreadsheet on my phone, an incoming text appeared.


**Ben Finley:** @ the merch counter. One of the trucks will be late.

**Carol Lynne Miller:** How late?

**Ben Finley:** They're in transit. An accident held up traffic. Don't know the ETA.

**Carol Lynne Miller:** Ok. Keep me updated if anything changes.

**Ben Finley:** No problem.


I headed over to the merch booth, situated in the

lobby, to see if they were done with the setup. Most of these older venues, like Rockman, didn't have stores because these buildings were built before selling merch was a thing. So the metal scaffolds didn't fit with the elegant, carved moldings of the classical architecture.

Two ladies in black t-shirts with badges pinned to them, hooked hangers with the McRiff and Savage Lyric logos printed on them. All black, though. No color. Nothing to entice women. I took out my phone, added merch variety to my research list, then texted Maurice with the info he'd requested.

I slipped my phone inside my back pocket and said, "Excuse me." The ladies stopped what they were doing and gave me their attention. "The merch truck is delayed, so make sure you leave room for more stuff to be added."

They thanked me for the heads-up and continued to work. I returned to the auditorium where Keith's band, "McRiff," played their set while the sound engineer made adjustments. Stage lights cast them in shades of magenta and green that changed in time with the music.

At the same time, cameras were being set up around the auditorium. It would be cool if we do a live broadcast of the concert. People would pay to watch. I took out my phone to jot that idea when an incoming text appeared.

**Charlie High Falutin' Stevenson:** Where the hell are you? I'm at your door knocking, and you aren't here.

**Carol Lynne Miller:** I'm at the venue working.

**Charlie High Falutin' Stevenson:** The concert you told me about?

**Carol Lynne Miller:** Yessiree.

**Charlie High Falutin' Stevenson:** :)

**Charlie High Falutin' Stevenson:** Can I come?

**Carol Lynne Miller:** If you don't mind me running off on you to check things out, then sure.

**Charlie High Falutin' Stevenson:** I guess I can handle that. ;) Where are you?

**Carol Lynne:** Midtown. @ Rockman Center.

**Charlie High Falutin' Stevenson:** Do I need a pass to get in?

**Carol Lynne Miller:** Yes. Lemme go talk to the guys at the front to have them make a pass for you.

**Charlie High Falutin' Stevenson:** Thanks, doll.

**Carol Lynne Miller:** np

Ugh. *Doll*. That sounded…generic.

My stomach's growl reminded me that I didn't eat. I headed to the front booth, made a guest pass for Charlie, and instructed them to give it to him upon his arrival.

Finally free to eat, I huddled in the corner, on the steps of a blue rollable ladder, and took the veggie hummus sandwich out of my canvas bag. I ate supper among the buzz of voices and rock music that echoed during a band's soundcheck in the auditorium.

* * *

My heart skipped a beat as a stocky, handsome man with a square jaw and short brown hair walked into the auditorium. He wore an electric blue t-shirt and black jeans, and searched around for a second until his eyes found mine. Grinning, Charlie sauntered up to me while his brown eyes traveled my body. "Look at us. We match."

I peered down at my outfit, then met his eyes. "I suppose so." Not really, but no need to be rude.

Charlie reached out and palmed my fire pendant. He brought his face closer, and the scent of his spicy cologne wafted up my nose. I restrained myself from running my face along his scruffy jaw to fully enjoy the experience. That would send the wrong message.

He angled the pendant around, studying it. "I like this. It suits you."

My forehead creased, and I asked, "How's that?"

He dropped it and met my eyes, "It looks like it's on fire but contained in this shape. Structured fire. You."

*Wow.* Insightful...and surprising. I accepted that Charlie thought of me as nothing more than a convenience when he needed it. My pride couldn't handle it. After our last hookup, I decided to end that part of our relationship while remaining on good terms.

He was my best friend's brother, so we needed to coexist in a way that didn't bring Sarah turmoil.

My phone buzzed with an incoming text that drew me out of my thoughts. The display read Ben Finley.

"Gotta run. The merch counter is having issues. Stay and enjoy the show."

Charlie's face fell for a split second until he arranged his features into a polite smile. "Sure thing."

What the hell was that about? I shot up from the metal steps of the rollable ladder and hurried over to the merch counter.

Maurice gestured with his hands while talking to the girls at the merch booth. The stand was packed since the last time I saw it, with posters and cups on display and more black t-shirts.

"Maurice," I said. "I know the color black is popular, but I think they're missing a huge demographic.

Women are also concert-goers, and women love color. These items cater to men."

He shrugged. "That's something you're gonna have to talk to the talent management about. I'm here to make sure everything's set up. But if you think it'll make a difference, then bring it up to them."

I ignored the negative tone of his words, took out my phone, and added it to my list. "Will do." I flashed a bright smile, walked away, and then texted Ben to see if he needed anything.

**Carol Lynne Miller:** Everything cool?
**Ben Finley:** Yeah. One of the band members showed up drunk and fought with a member from another band. But I separated them, so don't worry.

Dang. Scrawny Ben had to split up a fight between drunken rock stars? I hurried to the dressing rooms and found Keith's band, McRiff. They sat on a couch while chatting and searching through their gift baskets.

I knocked on the door, and their eyes shifted to mine. "Guys, I'm Carol Lynne Miller, the promoter. Just wanted to stop by and thank y'all for being here. If there's anything you need, let me or Ben Finley know."

They all acknowledged with a round of "all right." Keith wore an odd expression that I couldn't identify. I smiled at him and gave him a slight nod. Then I raised my hand in a parting gesture and left.

Well, that was awkward. Were Keith and I destined to be weird around each other? Shouting "fucker" at him while being half-naked didn't help.

I poked my head into the other dressing rooms in hopes of identifying who got into the fight, but they were standing around, stretching and laughing.

Was Ben honest about the fight, or had they simmered quickly? I wouldn't put it past him to lie about it. I might've been jaded, but people here liked to strut like peacocks. They weren't above lying to get ahead. Found that out while working in PR.

After making my rounds, I walked out from the back to the empty stage. People had started to file in. I scanned the crowd.

Charlie stood off to the side with a beer cup in one hand, and his arm slung around a brunette. Her white lace dress looked like she time traveled from the '80s. They stood close, he whispered something in her ear, and she giggled.

I snorted. Definitely deserved better than being a convenience. I shouldn't have given him a chance in the first place.

My bottom lip stung from the clamp of my teeth, so I let it go, buried the hurt, rushed backstage, and tried to ease the burn in my gut all the while. The show kicked off, and I didn't speak to Charlie for the night.

I made it home around 1:30 a.m. because I stayed behind to ensure there were no damages. Those repairs would cost extra.

I'd made more money from the two concerts than my yearly income in PR. Maybe a vacation was in order. I've always wanted to go to Spain or Italy because the food would be phenomenal. Then an idea struck and lit me with hope.

Better yet, I could *buy a house*.

# CHAPTER 5

CHARLIE

I'd roused about a minute before my lids opened. My arms were draped around my pillow. The clock on my side table read 10:42 a.m. Shit, half my morning had disappeared.

Lumbering into my en-suite, I flipped on the lights and squinted because my bloodshot eyes and five o'clock shadow were reflected in the LED vanity mirror.

If Dad saw me walking into the office like this, he'd lose his shit. Luckily it was Sunday, so I could get away with looking disheveled.

After my weekend routine, I dressed in khaki shorts and a white tank. Dragging my exhausted ass to the kitchen, I took the package of frozen berries from the freezer, the milk carton from the fridge, dumped every-thing in a blender, and made a smoothie.

While I sipped on my breakfast, I glanced at the pot lights and remembered taking the superintendent to court because the electricals in this building needed updating. It was one of the downsides to living in an apartment. Their inability to keep up with the needs of their technologically driven tenants had limited the enjoyment of occupancy. I bet they cried when everyone wanted the internet.

When the interior designer showed me her first mock-up, it was a Vegas-mess of black lacquer furni-ture, swatches of zebra-print rugs, and blue LED light-ing. I balked.

The walls ended up being painted off-white, and white roman shades hung from the windows. A rustic, light oak, covered the floors, and fake potted plants were sprinkled around the apartment to give it life.

Decorating the wall were framed pictures of me and my sibs on Martha's Vineyard, along with some recent additions. One was of us dancing together at Bri's wedding, and another was of me in the hospital, holding Sarah's babies. That was the closest to having babies as I would ever get.

I went into my bedroom, made my bed, grabbed

my phone, and scrolled to the woman who had been on my mind lately.

**Charlie Stevenson:** Are you up and at 'em?

**The Hippy:** Just woke up. Not used to it. Gonna have to, though.

**Charlie Stevenson:** Gonna have to if this is going to be your full-time gig.

**The Hippy:** Yep.

*Yep*? That was it? Just yep. She'd been quiet lately, and it bugged me. She was usually talkative and friendly, but recently...I don't know. She'd been down.

I had a feeling she couldn't get away from me fast enough last night. Was she too busy, or was it something I did?

The last time I saw her, the stage lights made her look like a rock princess. After that, I hadn't seen or heard a word from her for the rest of the night.

Understandable since part of her job involved putting out fires left and right. Would've been nice to spend some time with her, though.

**The Hippy:** I'm thinking of moving. I really don't like this place.

**The Hippy:** The paint is peeling, and the walls look

filthy. The heat doesn't come on until it's legally required to turn on. This means, if there's a cold spell, it's freezing in here. Maybe then I could convince Momma to move in.

**Charlie Stevenson:** Where would you go if you moved?

**The Hippy:** Don't know. Not far from the city, because my work is here, so maybe outside of it.

**Charlie Stevenson:** Brooklyn? Queens? Hell, the Bronx?

**The Hippy:** No. Outside of the Tri-state-area. Upstate. But close enough so that I can drive in quickly when I need to.

**Charlie Stevenson:** Country girl doesn't like the city life?

**The Hippy:** Not really. I'd like a place with a fire pit out back, and a fireplace inside would be nice.

**Charlie Stevenson:** So a house then?

**The Hippy:** You thought I meant that I wanted to live in another apartment?

**Charlie Stevenson:** Nah, just checking.

Actually, that was surprising. Carol Lynne wanted a house. She never mentioned settling down. I never figured her to be that type.

**Charlie Stevenson:** Need help? Send me a wish list, and I'll forward it to my real estate agent.

**The Hippy:** I don't know. I can just as well contact one myself. You have a lot on your plate anyway. I don't wanna be trouble.

**Charlie Stevenson:** No trouble, doll. I can easily do it after I get home from work.

**The Hippy:** Won't you be tired afterward? Look, it's ok. I'll contact a real estate agent myself.

Damn. Why the hell was she being so stubborn?

**Charlie Stevenson:** No problem, Shug. I don't mind. In fact, I'd love to help in any way I can. Send me pictures and your wish list, and I'll send it off to Nicolette.

**The Hippy:** Sigh

**The Hippy:** Ok, fine. I'll send you some pictures. The list will come later once I do research on what I want.

**The Hippy:** A little later today, ok?

**Charlie Stevenson:** No problem. I'll contact Nicolette to let her know that I have a new client for her.

Perfect. I could use this to spin a favor from Nicolette for the fundraiser. She could find us a luxury rental we could use as an item to bid on. And maybe I could use this as a way to repay Carol Lynne for the kindness she showed to my sister. Plus, Nicolette Peters was hot. Win-win.

**Charlie Stevenson:** Better yet, can you come over? We can review everything here and maybe conference Nicolette. What do you think?

A minute had gone by before she'd responded.

**The Hippy:** Naw. I was planning on usin' today to de-stress.

**Charlie Stevenson:** Does that entail anything specific?

**The Hippy:** Burnin' incense.

**Charlie Stevenson:** Bring it here. I love the way that stuff smells.

**The Hippy:** Really?? Which one do you like?

**Charlie Stevenson:** What was that one that looked like a matchstick?

**The Hippy:** Palo Santo.

**Charlie Stevenson:** That one. Can you bring a little extra so I can burn some myself after you leave? I'll pay you for it.

**The Hippy:** Really?? You like it that much?

**Charlie Stevenson:** Yes.

**The Hippy:** Ok, I bought a fresh batch yesterday. I can bring some. And I think there's a spare ceramic dish kicking around. You shouldn't burn it without the dish, or else there'll be problems.

**Charlie Stevenson:** I'll pay you. And tell me where you bought it so I can go there to check the place out?

**The Hippy:** Wow! You like it that much? For real?

**Charlie Stevenson:** Hahaha. Yes

**The Hippy:** Ok, I can tell you where to go. :evil grin:

**Charlie Stevenson:** :tongue sticking out emoji:

**The Hippy:** What time do you want me there?

**Charlie Stevenson:** In about 1 hr? We'll have lunch while we look through pics and discuss your list.

**The Hippy:** Ok. Sounds good.

Her spirits picked up marginally from what I could sense through the tone of her words. *Great.* I hated seeing her depressed. The fact that I cared left a weird feeling in my gut.

# CHAPTER 6

Her blonde hair hung loose, and her black pants were wide-legged, but fit her slim hips just right. Her ribbed, yellow tank molded her boobs nicely, but they were covered by a black cardigan.

"I wasn't expecting this," she said as she strolled around with wonder on her visage as she took in my apartment.

"Damn, was I that much of a chad that you expected a bachelor's pad?" I asked.

She affected her patented deadpan expression, winked, and said, "Yessiree," which made me chuckle. Her southern sayings were too cute, though I couldn't tell her that, or else she'd stop.

"Blame the look of this place on summer vacations. Dad took us to Massachusetts when we were kids, and it was some of the best times of my life."

Carol Lynne walked over to the window and said, "Sarah used to talk about your family vacations and how much fun you guys had. I even saw a few pictures of you on the beach."

The sun bathed the front of her body in light, making her glow like an angel. She had a quiet beauty. Unassuming but there.

I'd forgotten how much she knew about me through her friendship with my sister. She probably knew more about me than anyone outside my family, which made me uncomfortable because I didn't know much about her.

"You lived on a commune, right? Did it feel like you were at camp all the time?"

Carol Lynne half-turned, making her blonde hair shimmer, and tossed me a smirk that I didn't know how to interpret. Weird because I read body language for a living. Well, not exactly, but that was part of it. This woman threw me off my game.

"I'd never been to camp, so I couldn't tell ya what it was like. We did a lot of physical labor," Carol Lynne answered.

I went over to her, took her hand, and led her to the

sectional. She took off her cardigan, tossed it on the seat, and sat down. Her back was ramrod straight at first, but settled moments later.

Nervous? Weird.

I rested a foot on the coffee table and reclined with one arm behind my head. "What was the nature of your labor?" I prompted.

"The idea was that everything belonged to everyone, and we worked to maintain what we'd owned. In reality, we were more like cheap farmhands. Folks who live there, work different aspects of a farming business to produce organic almond butter."

"Take it, you didn't like living there?" I asked.

She paused and scrunched her glossy lips. "No. When I was a little girl, I saw them all like a pack of liars. Especially since they ostracized my mother. They'd preached the evils of city life," she paused, "But evil took up many forms. The owner, Lynnette McGreevy, in my opinion, is the devil incarnate."

My brows knitted together. "Isn't your mom still there? Why doesn't she leave?"

"Believe me, every time we'd talked, I begged her to come live with me, but she refused. I don't know. Living there for so long, then moving to this city would be like taking a fish out of water." She expelled a breath and did that calm breathing shit she taught Sarah while we were in the hospital. For stress.

*Shit.* I don't know what I would do if my sisters, or hell, even my mother, got stuck in that situation. So much I wanted to ask, but the nosedive in her mood warranted a change of subject.

I got up. "You want something to drink, Shug? Coffee, tea, water?"

"Water would be nice, thanks. I suppose Shug is my new name?"

I kept my expression neutral and tossed, "Yep," over my shoulder and went to the kitchen to grab two bottles of water from the fridge, came back, and handed one to her.

She accepted it with a slight hike in her lips that served as a smile and said, "Thank you." Then she twisted the cap off and took a swig, which put her pretty throat on display. It begged to be nuzzled.

I snapped out of my stupor and said, "One thing I'd meant to ask. Do all of you at the commune meditate and burn incense?"

Carol Lynne nearly spat out the water and gulped instead, which caused her body to convulse in a coughing fit.

I reached over and patted her back.

After she recovered, she pressed a hand to her

chest and said, "Sheesh, give a girl some warning before you ask funny questions."

I smiled, even though I wasn't sure what was funny about it. But if it cracked her up, I'd take it. I responded with, "Will do," to her request.

A smile played on her lips. "No, the meditation and incense burning was just me. My health-ed teacher in high school, Mrs. Katz, showed us how to do it as a relaxation technique. I took to it like a duck to water and did it ever since. I used to spend my discretionary money on incense and books. It drove Momma crazy." Her eyes turned dreamy, probably caught up in memory.

"What's discretionary money?" I asked.

Carol Lynne snapped her eyes back and said, "It's an allowance that the farm pays out to its workers for shopping. So Momma and I pooled most of ours for more expensive purchases. To keep costs down, we shopped at Goodwill. I snuck a dollar here and there to buy colorful hair ties and toys similar to the ones the kids brought to school. My notebooks cost seventy-five cents, and I was teased because we couldn't afford the more expensive Mead composition ones." She pursed her lips and dug her nail into the water bottle's label.

I was lucky enough to be born into a family who didn't worry about where our next meal came from. I didn't scrounge for clothing or anything I wanted, for that matter. Dad made us serve at soup kitchens during the holidays. It made me see how fortunate I was, so I didn't take it for granted.

Knowing how Carol Lynne started out and how she pulled herself out of it made me admire her even more. I'd seen how hard it was for people to get out—nearly impossible. Accomplishing that, took an iron will.

This woman. Couldn't get enough of her captivating face. Those downturned, chocolate-brown eyes were wise, like she was onto my bullshit.

Carol Lynne's narrowed eyes met mine. "What?" she asked in a slightly defensive tone. "Rich boy doesn't want to hear about shopping at Goodwill?"

I reared back and gaped. "I was thinking how cool you were, actually, until you just ruined it."

Her face fell, and red splotches showed on her neck. She put her bottle of water on the coffee table, grabbed her jacket, tablet, got up, and walked to the door. It took a second for me to realize what she was doing.

Rushing after her, I grabbed her arm. "Whoa, whoa, whoa. Come back. Sugar, I don't look down on you. Quite the opposite, actually."

She took a deep breath and looked down for a second before she gave her attention back to me.

Carol Lynne grimaced. "Sorry I overreacted."

I placed my hand under her chin and tipped her head up so that I could look into her brown eyes. "The only way I'll ever look down at you is physically." Bouncing on my tip-toes to make the point, I folded my arms around her and pressed a kiss on top of her head. "You're awesome. The way you worked yourself out of that situation is rare. We can't choose where we were born, but we can choose where we end up. And every-thing you'd done to end up where you are, is damned incredible." After another quick peck, I let her go and took her hand, kissed the back of it, and led her back to the couch.

"Now that we got that awkwardness out of the way, what should we do now?" Carol Lynne asked with a sheepish expression as she smiled.

We sat next to each other, and I rested an arm around her shoulder. It was an absentminded gesture. I just wanted her to feel better. She stiffened up at first, then relaxed into it.

"How about Pad thai for lunch?" I asked.

Carol Lynne smiled, which caused her eyes to sparkle, and she nodded.

I grinned at her enthusiasm for my suggestion and inspected to see if she was okay. She shifted her

# CHAPTER 7
CAROL LYNNE

Why the hell was Charlie staring at me so dang much? It weirded me out. Not to mention how touchy-feely he'd gotten. That was the kind of thing I was hoping to avoid and why being here wasn't a good idea. When I tried to storm out, I never expected him to stop me. I needed to find a way to leave without being rude.

At least we were having Pad Thai. I didn't have it in a while, and it was one of my favorites.

Should've held my tongue about wanting to buy a house. Now he was going to be all up in my business, probably calling or texting. And I'll need to work harder to put distance between us.

Unlocking the password screen on my tablet, I

scrolled through the photo library to the saved pics of cool homes.

Charlie picked up the remote from the coffee table, turned on the TV, and flipped through the channels until he got to the house-hunting show. Then he winked and said, "For inspiration."

I chuckled despite myself.

Charlie readjusted himself, so we sat side by side with our bodies touching. I hated the zing of energy that flowed from our connected parts. That electricity spread to my stomach and lower regions. His glittering chestnut eyes wandered down to my lips.

I scooted a smidge to put some necessary distance between us. Charlie's brows pulled together, and he frowned.

Pinning my attention to the notepad app on my tablet, I scrolled to the wish list I composed before I came. He scanned it then looked back up at me.

"Long list," he finally said, breaking the awkwardness between us.

"I'll be happy with a house with three bedrooms, a few bathrooms, a good-sized backyard, and a fireplace. I'm not too picky. I figure over the next coming years, I could renovate till it fits my needs exactly."

A slow, devilish smile spread on his face. "I'm sure we can find you something that's the right fit."

*Bastard.*

I rolled my eyes and ignored his double entendre. "When do you think we can call the real estate agent? Is she available on the weekend?"

His expression sobered, and for a split second, his eyes turned curious before he wiped it and answered, "Yes. She works on the weekends because people are home from work and have the time to house hunt."

I nodded. "Makes sense."

"Question," he said. "Why do you want a big back-yard? Planning on hosting a burning man?" That naughty-boy twinkle in his eyes shot tingles up my arms.

"I miss having a yard. I miss the earth. A fire pit would be really nice. I could barbecue on a grill and have a vegetable garden instead of buying veggies at the store. Then there's the decorating. So many flowers to choose from. Best of all, not having to ask the land-lord for permission every time I want to paint." So lost in my fantasy, I overlooked the intense study he gave me.

"You miss home," Charlie said after I'd finished my spiel.

He caught me. Well...no denying it, I guess. "Yeah, you could say that." My cheeks heated.

"How long have you been away from it?"

"I'm twenty-eight, so ten years. I left after high school graduation with a full-ride scholarship to MSU in Springfield. I got a job working at an off-campus cafe, and I also made scented candles and sold them at a craft store. So I rented an apartment with two girls. After that, I became so busy that I didn't have time to go back."

"You're a hard worker. My dad would've loved for my sisters to show the kind of gumption you had. They were both a little spoiled."

I narrowed my eyes. "I find that hard to believe. Sarah busts her ass for that pie business. She's not afraid of hard work. That was why I helped her to develop it in the first place. All she needed was a push in the right direction."

Charlie scoffed. "Dad gave her that yacht. It wasn't like she worked for years."

Anger ignited in my core for my friend. This rich bastard will inherit his father's multimillion-dollar company, and he moaned about a boat worth a fraction of that.

My nostrils flared. "That boat just sat there. Sarah turned it into a success. Maybe she hadn't worked for years at the same company, and maybe her dad gave her the boat but making a success out of nothing was no easy feat, Charlie."

He put his hands up in surrender. "Okay, I get it. Your loyalty to my sister can't be questioned." Asshole-ness colored his tone.

"It isn't a question of loyalty. It's about pissing and moaning when you have so much already."

Charlie's eyes narrowed, and his voice held an edge of anger. "I'm not pissing and moaning. Is it so wrong for me to feel some kind of way that my father gave Sarah an opportunity and makes me work like a fucking dog to earn mine?"

"As I said before, she earned success because she built that business from the ground up. She would have been successful even if your dad hadn't intervened."

"It was *given* to her. You want me to act like it didn't bother me?" Charlie no longer held an edge, he was full-on pissed.

"I'm not asking you to *act*. I'm asking you to be more supportive, or maybe just understanding. Sarah might have had help, but that didn't mean she wasn't willing to work hard."

Charlie stood, his hands fisted on his hips.

I got up, took my stuff, and marched to the door and he didn't bother stopping me this time.

I'd gotten what I wanted. But my throat burned, and my heart weighed a ton as I hurried out of the building.

# CHAPTER 8

On my couch, I browsed for interior color ideas on my laptop while folks found their dream home on TV. Charlie ghosted me since I left his apartment, so I was on my own. Again.

Gotta admit that I enjoyed his texts every few days to say the most random stuff. But there was silence since last week ever since he asked me over.

When I thought about how everything went down between us, I was torn. On one hand, I felt terrible for hurting him. But, on the other, his sister didn't have it easy. She fought to pull herself from the wake of a devastating loss. Why couldn't he understand that?

My phone binged on the coffee table with an incoming text.

**Sarah Stevenson**: Are you free? Can you come over to help look after the babies? Reese is on a job. I'm alone, and I haven't seen you in a while.

**Carol Lynne Miller:** Ok, puddin'. ;) When do you want me there?

**Sarah Stevenson:** ASAP. There will be chili and a glass of red wine in it for you.

**Carol Lynne Miller:** You had me at babysitting, but thanks for the food. Btw, red wine? You aren't supposed to be boozing it up around my godchildren.

**Sarah Stevenson:** Oh, quit your mother henning. And I'm not drinking. The wine was for you. I only drink water these days and the occasional charcoal lemonade.

**Carol Lynne Miller:** Ok, I'll be there ASAP, and we'll discuss this charcoal lemonade further when I see you.

**Sarah Stevenson:** Cool. Later gator. :p


Between her husband's catering business and her bistro, they were stocked with food. I don't think I'd seen Sarah cook since she'd started seeing Reese. Not that she cooked before him. I remembered eating frozen lasagna or frozen pizza at her place on many occasions.

That was why when she came over, I served home-made meals so she could've at least eaten something nutritious.

Sarah told me that she pursued a degree in culinary arts once when I was at her place for supper. Usually, people in that field were filled with a driving passion. My gut told me something was profoundly wrong.

Later, I found out that her fiancé was killed during an armed robbery and she suffered a miscarriage a few days after. Then everything clicked. Survivor's guilt overwhelmed her. I know a little something about that.

Years of me pushing her to move on with her life made her take that first step. But it wasn't until she met Reese that she changed.

I set them up on a blind date in the first place. I like to think of myself as Sarah's fairy godmother–if the godmother had chakra beads and smelled of patchouli.

Cutting off the TV, I grabbed my black leather purse, black cardigan from the closet and left to see my friend.

# CHAPTER 9

## CHARLIE

**Reese Malone:** Can't make it this morning, bro. On my way to the Catskills for a wedding. I'll be gone all day.

**Charlie Stevenson:** Es is alone with the kids then?

**Reese Malone:** Yeah.

**Charlie Stevenson:** Cool. I'll let her know that I'll be over. I can look after your trolls while she naps. :p

**Charlie Stevenson:** But after my game.

**Reese Malone:** K

Shutting off the phone, I tucked it into the pocket of my gym bag.

"Is Reese comin'?" Colin Brady asked and tossed the basketball from one hand to the other. His hair was swept back. He was clean-shaven and tall like

Reese. Unlike Reese, whose resting bitch face made him look pissed most of the time, Colin's playful gleam reminded me of Sammy, Reese's younger brother.

"Nah, just us today," I answered.

Colin tossed me the ball, then threw out his lanky arms to guard. I bounced the ball while walking forward, spun around him, and powered towards the basket. The layup bounced off the backboard and fell effortlessly through the hoop.

"Two," I announced.

Colin scrambled for the ball, bounced it outside the three-point boundary line, and shot it. It sailed in an arch and fell through the hoop.

"Three," he said with a shit-eating grin.

We bathed in sweat by the time the game was over. I beat Colin ninety-seven to ninety-four because I lucked out when he missed a throw. But, most times, he won, which I blamed on his youth.

"Wanna grab some lunch?" he asked while he toweled the sweat from his face.

"Can't. Reese is gone for the day, so my sister is by herself and I'm gonna help her babysit."

"All right. See ya next week." We clapped hands, then locked in a hold before letting go. Colin turned and strode off the court towards his parked car with his duffle bag slung over his shoulder.

I fished the phone out of the bag's side pocket and texted my sister.

**Charlie Stevenson:** I'm coming over.

**Es Malone:** Cool. The more, the merrier. ;)

# CHAPTER 10
### CAROL LYNNE

Sarah opened her door and placed a finger on her lips in a shushing gesture. I played along and tiptoed into her magnificent apartment.

This place struck me every time I came. The windows spanned floor to ceiling, let so much light in. Red-bricked walls gave it a lofty feel, and the beams and flooring added elegance. Reese scored big time when he bought it.

Sarah and I stood in her entranceway, hugging for a while. We didn't have much time to hang out after the babies were born, and I missed her something fierce.

The dark circles under her gray eyes and frizzy strands that came loose from her bun sent a bolt of pity through my system. She didn't even tuck the hem of her jean shirt into her black pants like she used to. Sarah was always beautiful, but her vibe screamed she could drop at any second.

I should do more to help, since I no longer had an office job.

She led me to a barstool by the kitchen island. A pitcher of what I figured was charcoal lemonade sat between two empty glasses on the counter. The promised chili filled a glazed blue pot, and white bowls surrounded it. Off to the side was a dessert plate filled with Napoleons.

We took our seats, and she ladled chili into the bowls. The spicy scent tickled my nose.

"What have you been up to?" she whispered while serving.

"Well, there's something I need to tell you."

Sarah raised her brows, "Oh?"

"I'm thinking of buying a house outside the city. Somewhere upstate, but close enough to drive to work."

Her brows shot up, and she smiled. "Wow. Cool! I take it that everything is going well with the promotion business?"

Her reaction made me smile. "Yessum, far better than I thought. Had I known then what I know now, I would've gotten into the concert promotion game sooner. It's fun. I love the buzz of energy, and making arrangements."

Sarah nodded, picked up her spoon, and gestured with it while she spoke. "That's the thing, though. Everything you'd gone through before served as training for your life now. Chances are, you would've never been such a good promoter if you didn't know the ins and outs of PR."

Sarah was wiser than most people gave her credit. In an odd way, she reminded me of Momma. Although they looked nothing alike, there was something similar in their personalities. It drew me to her from the very beginning and was the reason I went to bat against Charlie. I'd defend my mother to the end.

"Never thought of it that way. Makes me feel better for sticking it out at Sutter for that long. At least it doesn't feel like a giant waste of time," I said, then ate a spoonful of chili. To my surprise, it wasn't as spicy as I thought it would be.

Sarah nodded. "So, tell me about this house you want to buy. Did you decide on anything yet?"

"Not yet. I just made a wish list, and I saved a bunch of pictures from PixelPost so that I can show the real estate agent what I'm looking for."

She swallowed her bite, then asked, "What's on your wishlist?"

"A fireplace—"

A knock on the door interrupted me. Sarah scrambled off the barstool, ran to answer it before the person could knock again and wake the babies. She opened the door and whispered something I didn't catch.

The person entered, and my stomach dropped.

Charlie wore a sweat-stained gray tank that displayed his muscular body and black basketball shorts. With his wet hair, and black gym bag that hung at his side, I figured where he came from.

His happy face suddenly dropped to a frown when we locked eyes.

My stomach bottomed out, and brought my appetite with it. Heavens to Betsy, he was still pissed!

Charlie said, "Sorry, Es, didn't know you had company. I'll leave you two alone."

She rested a hand on his arm and said, "Oh, come on! You two can't be in the same room with each other? Is it that bad?"

Sarah was oblivious to our relationship. More than likely, she probably thought we didn't have much of one. She was right. I'd never told her about our previous hookups because that would've been a weird convo.

He came further into the room while scratching his head and his face fixed in a grimace.

I could do this. I could be an adult. Heck, I had to, as with so many things prior. Like when I found out that he didn't believe in monogamy or commitment. I suppressed my need to avoid him because he was my best friend's brother, and it wouldn't be right to fight with her family.

I pasted a smile on my face and sat straighter. "Hi, Charlie, there's plenty of chili left. Would you like some?"

Charlie cast me the slightest glance, then addressed his sister. "Actually, Es, can I grab a quick shower?"

Sarah's eyes rounded, and her face froze momentarily. She looked at me, then looked back at him and stammered, "Yeah, sure. You know where the bathroom is."

He thanked her, walked past the two of us, rounded the corner to the bathroom, and locked the door. We stared in his direction for a second, then Sarah pounced.

"What happened between you two?"

Since we fought about her, I couldn't very well tell her what went down without hurting her feelings. And as hurt as I was, I didn't want her thinking poorly of her brother.

"Oh, who knows. He gets his tail in a knot over the

dumbest things.  But I should really leave.  He came here to see you." I got up from the stool and grabbed my bag. "We'll catch up later."

She frowned, "Why can't you stay? I haven't seen you in forever."

"We'll catch up again. Promise I won't stay away for too long." I avoided answering her question and hugged her. "Love ya, darlin'." Then I scooted my behind outta there.

A pang of regret squeezed my chest because a few moments ago I decided to be mature about this. But in reality, this didn't involve just me. Sarah would be affected too, and I didn't want her to stress. If I'd stayed, she would have definitely sensed something went down between us. With two babies to look after, she didn't need that.

Besides, if she had questions, she could direct them to her brother. He could better explain why we couldn't be in the same room.

# CHAPTER 11

A veggie burger awaited on the coffee table while I switched the channel on TV to *House Hunters*. Moving to an island would be cool, but probably no work in my line of business. Might be something to think about for retirement, though.

An urgent knock at the door snapped me from my thoughts. Keith? Hadn't seen him since the concert, and I wasn't even sure he was in town.

I opened the door to Charlie. His blue jeans and plain black t-shirt molded to his well-developed body. The bouquet of Blanket Flowers which he extended looked like tiny suns.

My mouth fell open, and my heart fell to my stomach. Never thought I'd see him again, especially holding flowers.

"May I come in?" He asked in a conciliatory tone.

I stepped aside. Charlie walked in and checked out my place. His gaze snagged on the wind chimes that hung from the ceiling.

"I came over to thank you for not telling Es how I felt about the yacht. And I brought these. They reminded me of you. Sunshiny." He held up the flowers.

Wait...what? Did he think I was some mean witch who would deliberately harm my friend? What did he take me for?

My eyes narrowed, and I crossed my arms. "I would never hurt Sarah. No matter what you might think of me, I would never do that."

Charlie frowned and lowered the bouquet. "What do you mean, what I might think of you?"

"Why do you think I would say something to hurt Sarah? Did you think I was that heartless?"

His eyes rounded. "No. I...look. I know how it is when women get together and talk. They share things they shouldn't."

My forehead scrunched, "They did? Where did you get that from?"

Charlie answered, "TV. They talk about a man's

size, his ass, and what positions are his favorite. You know...shit like that."

At first, I gawked at him like he grew two heads. But then, he wasn't that far off. I never overshared, but I guess some women did.

"Okay, maybe some women have those kinds of relationships, but not everyone. Anyway, why in the world would I tell your sister about your penis? File that under the category of *ew*. And what TV shows are you watching?"

He rolled his eyes. "You know, girl shows. I need to learn how to relate better to women...for work."

Still regarding him like he was nuts, I asked, "And you think dick shows would do that? If a lawyer talked to a client about someone's dick—"

"Okay, okay. I watch it because it's entertaining and hot." His cheeks stained.

Charlie's confession drained my steam and I didn't have a chance against the smile that broke out. Gorgeous moron.

Taking the flowers, curtsied a thank you and gestured to the living room with them. "Care to stay? I was fixin' to have supper. Want me to rustle up another burger for you?" Manners that Momma had ingrained didn't allow me to be rude.

Charlie grinned. "Sure, if it's no trouble."

"Not at all." I grabbed an extra patty from the

freezer and placed it in the pan that sat on the stove from earlier use. It surprised me that he stayed. Reckoned he would've apologized and left.

Taking the white pitcher vase from the overhead cupboard, I filled it with water. Then I unwrapped the flowers from their green tissue paper, stuck them inside the vase, and set it on my desk.

"Someone sent you flowers?" He asked in a defensive tone.

I glanced over my shoulder and caught Charlie stink facing my roses on the TV stand. "I sent those to myself for a job well done after the concert."

Charlie's face fell and I returned to preparing his meal.

"Any luck finding a place?" He asked while settling on the couch. Something about that reminded me of Sarah.

I spoke over the sizzle from the pan. "Naw. Been saving pictures from PixelPost of features that I would like. Anything to drink? Bottled water, ginger ale, Kombucha sweet tea?"

"Water, thanks. What's Kombucha?"

"It tastes like cider and has health benefits. Wanna try it?"

After a moment of consideration, he answered, "Okay, why not?"

I chose the clear, mild one from the variety of flavors in the fridge because the harder stuff would turn him off completely.

When I handed it to him, he took it with dancing eyes. He cracked the cap open, took a sip, then examined the label. "Not bad. Swear, I learn something new every time I'm around you."

I went back to the burger and said over my shoulder, "That's because we have different interests."

Charlie said, "Nice to learn new things, though. It's refreshing."

Interesting way of looking at it. I hiked my brows and fried his burger.

After about five minutes, his burger was ready. I loaded it with toppings and brought the plate over to him.

He took a bite and beamed. "Wow. It tastes like regular meat. I'll be honest, I had my doubts."

I sighed, picked up my plate from the coffee table, and settled next to him. "Never know until you try. And, it's healthy to change your diet every once in a while." I took a bite of burger and chewed.

Charlie blinked, "I didn't think that vegans ate cheese. But clearly, you like it."

I shrugged. "Vegans don't. I'm not a vegan. I just like to eat veggie foods."

His brows raised. "Why?"

I swallowed, then said, "I grew up on a farm where we grew an abundant supply of veg. My fondest little-girl memories were of me and Momma pickin' them. She was one of the few cooks who lived on River Run. I'd help her in the kitchen. Now, I could whip up anything out of a few vegetables. Plus, I love to cook Momma's recipes. It feels like she's right here with me."

His eyes softened, and it made me feel like bees were circling. Refocusing on supper, I took another bite while watching TV.

"I get that. When Mom and Dad were still married, Sarah would put together family dinners on Sundays. She'd search through the internet for recipes, then cook us these awesome meals. Mom and Dad weren't getting along, so tensions were high, but the food–" He shook his head.

"Food has that way about it. Preparing it can summon memories, as well as eating it." My chest pulled tight while sweet flashbacks played in my mind.

"I never thanked you," he said.

That made me look at him. "For what?"

"For looking after my sister, the way you had."

My brow furrowed. "Looking after her? Sorry, I don't follow."

"When Reese was in the hospital, you stayed with her and helped her with those breathing exercises. And even before that, when you helped her set up the pie business. If it hadn't been for you, my sister would still be lost."

I blinked, taken back. No one knew how much work it took to help someone brought low by life. Shocking that he understood that enough to appreciate it.

A lump formed in my throat. I drew in breath and said, "Thank you."

His smile was tender. "I know you love her. But, why did you do all that? With the business, I mean?"

I studied the rim of my plate. "She reminds me of my mother."

Charlie's head jerked. "Really? How so?"

"Well, not in looks. Momma is a short woman with a round figure, and she has light brown hair as opposed to Sarah's dark brown. But Momma's story was tragic, like Sarah's. Lynette McGreevy slept with Momma's boyfriend, my father. Then she got pregnant with my father's baby. He took off, leaving Momma and me behind. Lynette treated Momma super shitty ever since. To appease her so we could stay, she named me after her."

Charlie's expression morphed into a variety of

emotions as I told my story. "Wow. That was downright fucked up. But how did she remind you of Es?"

"Sarah needed help to get out of the hole she crawled into. So does Momma. The difference is that Momma accepts her lot and won't crawl out."

"Remembered you'd said that you offered for her to move in."

I dipped my chin. "So many times, I'd lost count. She won't accept help. Besides that, I live in New York, the mecca of the corporate world they brainwashed her to despise." My voice sounded dejected.

He stopped eating, raising his head and brows. "They brainwashed you?"

I huffed. "Not the brainwashing where they stick you in a room, put a metal hat on your head with a bunch of wires attached to a machine."

He asked through a bite. "Isn't that called shock therapy?"

Was it? I shrugged. "Anyway, they mentioned things here and there repeatedly to reinforce their beliefs. Before you knew it, those beliefs became your own. And you really believed it if you had a rough go of corporate life."

He sipped his kombucha, then asked, "So, how did you turn out different?"

"Do I seem different to you?"

He shrugged. "You're here, living and working in the *mecca of the corporate world*. Obviously, their brain-washing didn't work on you."

I swallowed my last bite of burger. "Their downfall was allowing kids to attend public schools. It was ideal for the parents because it freed up their time to complete their daily work quota. Because of that, public school influenced the way that we looked at our lives. It made us dream up possibilities for our future. In fact, all the kids who grew up on the farm left to pursue better lives."

"How does the farm sustain loyal members if the kids leave?" He sipped his kombucha.

"The folks who want to join are drifters. Well, most of 'em, anyway. The ideology is attractive to those who own nothing. When they join, they own all that land, food, and shelter. Pretty much everything a person needs. In Momma's case, I reckon also because she'd built a life where she didn't have savings, so she couldn't get out."

He shook his head and said, "Wow," then placed his empty plate on the coffee table, downed his bottle of kombucha, and stood up. "Shug, I hate to eat and run, but you just gave me an idea of how to solve something that had been bugging me. I need to go to the office."

Resting my plate on the coffee table, I got up. "Ah, okay. Glad I could help."

Charlie placed his arm around my shoulder, pulled me close, then kissed my forehead. "Listen, if you hadn't gotten around to house hunting, I still want to help."

The butterflies erupted in my stomach. "Yeah, sure," I said, flustered.

He walked to the door, turned back to me, and said, "Thanks for dinner. It was delicious. I'll buy next time." Charlie winked, and it made me melt.

A mischievous grin spread across his face when he walked out the door.

# CHAPTER 12
## CHARLIE

Flipping on the lights in my office, I parked my ass in the chair and keyed open my desk drawer. The box of condoms hidden under my notebooks made me pause. Hadn't used them in a few weeks. I dug around until I found the reference notebook.

Someone knocked on the door then pushed it open. With a hand on the knob, Dad stuck his head inside.

"Saw you come in. Great that you're working on the weekend and showing initiative. Anything particular on your mind?"

I answered while thumbing through my notebook. "Reviewing liabilities, something I wanted to check."

"So research then?" he asked.

I paused my perusal and focused on him. His face was lit with an anticipatory gleam. "Everything all right? Shouldn't you be with Connie instead of working on the weekend?"

"Connie is with her son, Dennis, in Arizona. His wife had given birth to a little girl last week, so Connie's there helping them out."

I hiked my brows. "Wow! Congrats to her. What's the baby's name?" I asked.

"Olivia," he answered with a smile. He loved babies, especially girls, judging by the way he doted on my sisters.

*But never on me.* My jaw twitched.

Burying whatever emotions hit, I said, "Olivia. Beautiful name. I'll send the baby a gift." I jotted a note of that on the legal pad sitting on my desk.

Dad's jaw ticked and something flickered in his eyes. "That would be nice son, I'm sure they'll appreciate it."

"No problem." My smile was tight and I resumed my search.

Dad walked deeper into my office and with his hands stuffed in his designer pockets, he asked, "Now tell me what's really wrong."

I nearly rolled my eyes but managed not to. "Nothing's wrong, just searching for a procedure. Wrote it down somewhere in my reference book a million years ago and I'm trying to find it."

"Anything else?" Dad pressed.

My brows drew down, and my tone came off defensively. "Anything else? What are you talking about?"

He examined me for a second before he answered. "Something came over you when I mentioned Olivia."

*Shit*. He noticed. I triggered his finely honed bullshit detector with my passing thoughts. It was what made him a brilliant attorney but hell for his kids. We couldn't get away with shit. I tried to keep my feelings in check, but somehow he'd caught it and badgered the truth out of me. Swear, if he was a gambling man, he'd clean up.

"Nothing came over me, Dad. I was just surprised. I'm happy for Connie. It's cool to have a grandchild, and Olivia is a beautiful name. Es will be happy when she hears."

My sister had gotten pretty close to Connie while she was pregnant, and had to stay at Dad's. Reese went through dangerous shit that his crazy ex brought on, involving the mob. Luckily that situation ended well, but it had gotten hairy for a time. And during that time, Dad and Connie stepped in.

"Yes, I should tell your sister the next time I talk to her. By the way, have you spoken with her lately?"

I rolled my eyes. "Spent most of the day at her place helping with the kids since Reese was away. Why do you ask?"

"Just checking. Well, I'll leave you to get your work done. See you later," he took off, closing the door behind him.

Wiggling my clenched jaw from side to side, it loosened. It annoyed me to no fucking end that he had to make sure I did the right thing. As though he didn't trust that I would.

Biting back my resentment, I returned my attention to my reference book and found the entry. It referred to a specific textbook in my Guide to Law and Practice library on pre-incorporation contracts and liabilities. It made me wonder how far along was Carol Lynne's application for incorporation, or if she started one at all.

I took the phone out of my back pocket, scrolled to Carol Lynne's contact name, and changed it.

**Charlie Stevenson:** Shug, quick question.

**Shug Miller:** Shoot.

**Charlie Stevenson:** Did you file articles of incorporation?

**Shug Miller:** Yes. Your dad helped me set it up.

Didn't know that. Well, I guess he would since he seemed to be a fan of hers.

**Charlie Stevenson:** Really? Why didn't I know this?

**Shug Miller:** We weren't on the best of terms, so I didn't inform you.

I winced.

**Charlie Stevenson:** Sorry I wasn't there to help you, Shug.

**Shug Miller:** Thank you, kindly.

She must have said the last part with a slight nod and a Southern accent. Cute. A smile grew on my face.

**Charlie Stevenson:** Btw, what did you name the corporation?

She took a moment longer to respond, which deepened my curiosity.

**Shug Miller:** Promise you won't laugh?

**Charlie Stevenson:** Promise

**Shug Miller:** Firelight Productions

It didn't make me laugh, it made me confused.

**Charlie Stevenson:** Why "firelight?"

**Shug Miller:** When I was a girl, we gathered around a campfire. This one guy who lived there, named Raul, sang with a guitar. There were other singers too, but he was the guy in charge of organizing the gatherings.

**Shug Miller:** Putting together concerts means that I took over Raul's role.

**Shug Miller:** It also reminded me of where I started.

**Charlie Stevenson:** All of that sounds beautiful, baby. Proud of you.

After re-reading what I wrote, I might've laid it on too thick. A pang of regret ran through me, but my sentiments were genuine. She overcame so much to get where she is today, and I *am* proud. Shug carved a place for herself on a grander scale than how she grew up. She rocked, in every sense of the word.

A chuckle popped out of my mouth.

After accomplishing what I came here to do, I bounced.

# CHAPTER 13

CAROL LYNNE

While browsing for aesthetic ideas for the Christmas concert early Sunday morning, my phone buzzed with a text notification. Someone knocked on the door at the same time.

Forgetting the phone, I rose and headed to the door, peeked through the peephole, and let out a groan before opening it.

"I come bearing gifts," Charlie said as he held up a small paper bag and a tray which held two coffee cups.

The scent of coffee mixed with baked treats filled my nose and aroused my appetite. I grinned, moved to the side, and gestured for Charlie to come in with a wave of my arm.

"Mornin'. This is a surprise."

"You're kidding, right? I texted that I was coming," he rested our breakfast on the coffee table and settled on the couch.

"Was that you? I just received it." I picked up my phone, unlocked it, and opened the text screen, which read, "Open up, Shug."

I continued, "Yep, as you were knockin'." My eyes found a smile on his sexy lips. "What?"

"It's cute when your accent slips."

"Does that sometimes, I guess." I hid the heat on my cheeks by pulling the coffee table towards the couch, then bought more time by going to the kitchen to grab dessert plates and a few napkins.

Refusing to be derailed by my stalling tactics, he said, "Don't be afraid to let loose with it, Shug. It's charming." His eyes twinkled as he took the crockery from me and tabled them.

I squeezed in to sit beside him and caught his barely audible groan when I passed by.

What do I do with all these compliments? He'd complimented me before. It was just that he didn't mean it, like he fed me lines. Now, I don't know. It felt different. Sincere.

I bit my lip and focused on the bag. "What did you

bring?" Reaching in, I pulled out the mystery pastry. "Cronuts! Lordy, I love Cronuts. How did you know?"

He accepted the extended bag, took out the last confectionary, then crumpled the empty bag in one hand. Shrugging, he said, "Asked Es."

My brows lifted. "You asked your sister what my favorite breakfast was?"

"Yes, I texted her before I came over."

I bit my lip. Now Sarah will ask questions the next time we talk. I said nothing to her about our relationship... or whatever this was, because it wasn't a big deal.

"So, what did you have in mind today?" I didn't want to be rude, but why was he here?

"I thought we could go over your list and get you set up with my real estate agent, Nicolette Peters."

I agreed while savoring the pastry's flakiness. Then I reached for the coffee, snapped back the tab, and sipped from the warm cup.

Why couldn't he just pass my number to Nicolette so that she could call me instead of going through all this? The voice in the back of my head said he wanted to use the list to get closer to me.

The other, cynical voice said he wanted to get closer to Nicolette. That was the voice I needed to listen to because it kept me safe. Confusing Charlie's friendliness for anything more would be hazardous to my heart. My shoulders slumped.

"What were you up to before I came in? I heard tapping coming from your keyboard echoing from down the hall. This place doesn't offer much privacy, does it?" He asked, pulling me away from my dejected thoughts.

I swallowed my bite. "No, and that's one of the reasons from the laundry list of many why I want to move. I was doing some research earlier, trying to figure out what kind of show I can put on at Christmas. I mean ... what I can offer to entice people to attend, while not breaking the bank."

He shook his head. "That's a tall order. Never thought of that sort of stuff before. Interesting, though."

"That's because I'm the only concert promoter you've met." Half my lips turned up.

Charlie chuckled and sipped from his cup. Suddenly, his eyes grew wide. "Right about that. Hey, I've been meaning to ask, could you coordinate our fundraiser?"

Didn't they have people who handled that? "I might could, but it goes against the grain. Corporate events and all that."

He grinned, and his eyes dropped to my lips for a split second. "Sugar, you are the head of your own corporation. If you don't consider yourself evil, what makes you figure we are?"

I paused before taking a bite and tossed him a begrudging lip quirk. "Touché."

"By the way, didn't you once tell me the commune sold almond butter? Wasn't that a business as well?"

"Yes, but it's a nonprofit."

He halted from taking another bite, arched his brow, and said, "Interesting."

Oh? I leaned in. "Interesting, how?"

"Nonprofits receive income from donations, so I was curious how a nut butter company supports itself."

"Do you think they're shady?" I asked.

"Not until I examine the facts, but it seems they aren't reporting profits from what it sounds like."

I snorted, "Huh. Lynette McGreevy, a criminal. I could see that."

Charlie continued, "Also, a nonprofit is a type of corporation. Odd they're denouncing what they are," he added a tidbit I'd often wondered about. "Did they like you? Because you were more business-minded, I mean."

I wrinkled my nose. "Not really. They tolerated me. I was my mother's daughter, after all."

He lowered his brows. "And being treated like that was preferable to living in the city?"

I admitted my hope. "If I buy a house, she might decide to leave. That was the plan, anyway."

Charlie's gaze shifted to eagle-eyed like something was churning in the back of his mind. Finally, he nodded and said, "Maybe. If we find something nice, it could attract her."

"Reckon, if I take lots of pictures, I can go there and show 'em to her. Then I'll invite her to come. Been missin' her something fierce anyway, so it's time for a visit. Two birds, one stone."

"Sounds like a plan, Shug," he said.

For the rest of the time, we looked through pictures on PixelPost for ideas of what I wanted–a farmhouse with three bedrooms with a spacious backyard. A lanai with a fire pit would be lovely in the winter, but it's not definite. I could add that in a few years.

Charlie asked to see my lease. I dug it out from the files in my drawer and handed it to him. He scanned the paper and said, "Says it's up in three months."

"That should give me enough time to plan a show and start packing."

He chuckled, "Packing? You're jumping the gun, Shug. You don't have a house to move into yet."

I glanced around my apartment, making notes of things I could box. "If I pack early, the move will be easier. Waiting for the last minute, tossing everything in boxes willy-nilly, and losing things along the way would cause stress. Ah hell, it's giving me hives thinking about it."

My accent might have slipped because his eyes creased.

"You can still casually pack while making your show priority number one, so you won't break out in hives."

That suggestion slowed my roll. "Makes sense, I guess. How are you so good at calming me?"

He grinned. "I'm a lawyer, Sugar. It's my job."

Unease marred my smile because I wasn't a fan of the heat that ran through my body. Nope, not one bit.

Charlie stood suddenly, ruining the mood. "Gotta get going, babe. I have to do prep for the week." He walked to the door, and I followed. After he opened it, he said over his shoulder, "Thanks for having me over."

"Thank you for breakfast, and thanks for your advice with the other stuff."

"My pleasure, Shug." He swung open the door and took off just as Keith came out of his apartment. He watched Charlie's retreating back, then at me with a puzzled expression.

I tried not to be offended, but dang, lost that battle because it stung my pride. Before Charlie, I nursed an unrequited crush on Keith. He didn't have the vaguest interest, so I gave it up. But honestly, what was his problem anyway? My smile was tight-lipped, and I gave him a chin nod.

"Didn't know you rolled that way," he said.

"What way?" I asked, genuinely baffled.

"Straight."

# CHAPTER 14
### CHARLIE

Sitting at my dining table while reading the laptop screen, I scanned my to-do list while chowing down on a bowl of chili, bought from Greenery Organic Grocers on the way home from Shug's. Thanks to her, it seemed like I'd developed a taste for healthy food. It made me feel–I don't know–nurtured. Never knew how good it felt until we hung out.

Filled with optimism over how our breakfast went, I reckoned our new friendship would work. Shug didn't want anything from me, like most women. In fact, I had to force my help on her. Now that I understood her better, I needed to be crafty about offering help because she would reject it if she thought it was done out of pity.

That shit she told me about the farm business piqued my curiosity. I should poke around to see what was their deal because what Shug said left a sour taste in my mouth. But, then again, if I found out they were doing illegal shit, what recourse would I have? If I reported them to the IRS, her mother and the rest of those people would be kicked out on the street, which didn't sit well with me either.

Not to mention, her mother would face the wrath of her community leaders. So why she continued to stay was beyond me. But I'd bet the reason Carol Lynne thought she'd stayed was not the real reason. Can't put my finger on what tripped my alarm, but I don't know. It was a hunch.

I got up, went to the kitchen sink to rinse the spoon and bowl, and placed them in the dishwasher.

Someone knocked on the door. Rushing to wipe my hands, I dashed to the door and looked through the peephole. With a smile, I opened the door to find Bri and Troy. Greeting them, I held the door open for them.

Troy, who wore a black polo shirt, cargo pants, and sandals, strode ahead of my sister.

Bri gave me a quick hug and said, "We were in the neighborhood and wanted to drop by." Her white jeans and billowy brown top made her look runway model-beautiful as usual.

Troy added over his shoulder, "Yeah, we thought you could use a break from your Sunday prep."

It had been a while since I'd seen my sister. Our lives had drifted apart since they'd tied the knot. Bri used to text, filling me in on family gossip. Lately, she hadn't been around, which I'd attributed to her newlywed status.

Of my sisters, she was my favorite. Not that I didn't love Es, but Bri and I shared a natural bond. She gave a damn about me. *No one else had.* We grew closer after Es detoured into Zombieland after her fiancé and baby died and was unresponsive for years.

"A little one," I agreed out of politeness. I took a seat at one end of the couch and Troy on the other end, with Bri stationed between.

"How have you been?" Bri asked as her legs fidgeted.

Nervousness. Why was she nervous?

"Same old, same old. Work, home, rinse, and repeat." I smirked at them.

Bri arched her flawless brow. "Really? Es told me you asked what Carol Lynne's favorite breakfast was," she stated like she dropped the mic.

I cleared my throat. "She wants to move, and I'm helping her find a place."

"Can't she find a real estate agent to help with that?" Bri asked.

"She could, but I'll hook her up with one who's good at negotiating prices. I'm acting as her sounding board since Es is too busy with the babies to help."

"So there's nothing going on between you two?" Troy spoke up for the first time."

Why was it their business? Even if Carol Lynne and I had a thing, so what?

I ground down on my jaw, then deadpanned, "Naw, got other women who take care of that." Safe to say, there was no love loss between us since I'd been fucking his ex, Amberly.

Troy's face morphed to granite, and he peered at me with his ice-blue eyes. I would've found it creepy if I couldn't seriously kick his ass.

"Ah, we came by because we needed to tell you something before we spoke to dad." Bri put in with a shaky voice.

"What?" My guard shot up and my eyes narrowed on my sister.

"I'm pregnant. Due on the twenty-fifth of April," she beamed.

My mouth dropped open. I let go of the breath I'd

held and folded Bri in a hug. Then I shook Troy's hand in congratulations. He shook my hand with the enthusiasm of being forced to proofread a pile of contracts.

I said to my sister, "My God, I'm going to be an uncle again. Did you tell Es and Mom?" "Mom already knows. Dad and Es are next," she said, surprising me further. She was closer to our mother than the rest of us, which said little because our actress mother was a difficult person to get close to. They shared an interest in fashion.

We spoke for a bit longer, although my sister and I carried much of the conversation before they'd left. After they were gone, I grabbed my phone and broke the news to Carol Lynne, but told her not to mention it to Es because Bri didn't tell her yet.

She responded with:


**Shug Miller:** Thankfully, she didn't see my phone because she had just left.

**Charlie Stevenson:** For real?

**Shug Miller:** Yessir. Spent some time over here. Her kids loved this place, btw. Probably because it's colorful.

**Charlie Stevenson:** I bet they'll love your new house even more. ;)

**Shug Miller:** Fingers crossed. :)

# CHAPTER 15

Friday afternoon found myself at my desk, suffering the mind-numbing task of entering information from my legal pad into the affidavit template on my laptop.

Normally, I avoided lawyer shows on TV. But I can tell you one thing about lawyering. Glamorous and exciting, it wasn't. My only excitement was my highlighter ink running out.

Sometimes, I wandered around the building with a document in hand, as though I ran an errand, but I was really stretching my legs. Unlike Dad, I tried not to bring work home, who always did because he took refuge in it. Since I'm not hitched, I don't need an excuse to dodge headaches.

Wouldn't mind the work if it entailed helping people, not businesses. This branch of the legal system seemed cold…soulless.

The ringing of my phone snapped me out of my thoughts.

**Amberly Davidson:** Overtime?

I picked up the phone and smiled at her text. Been a while. Another incoming message lit the screen while my thumb hovered over the keys.

**Shug Miller:** Are we still on for tonight, or are you busy?

Troy barged into my office without knocking. "Rough day?" he asked.

"Long one. So, what's up?" I asked, so he could say what he needed to, then get the hell out of my office. His boring-ass tan pants, a white shirt, and a brown tie and combover made me puzzle over what my sister saw in him.

Amberly Davidson was the cause of our mutual hostility. She was his live-in girlfriend until he cheated on her with Bri. He was pissed that we hooked up, but couldn't say anything without provoking the ire of my family.

My chest squeezed. Amberly was the epitome of sweetness and deserved better than our hook-up sessions.

Troy shrugged. "Bri has morning sickness, and she's irritable."

My smile had a hint of assholery behind it. "She'll be emotional. It runs in the family, judging by Sarah and Mom." I tried to scare him for kicks.

"Guess, I can always say I have work to do or something and hide out in the home office," he laughed.

And leave my pregnant sister alone to fend for herself? *Nice.* What a gem?

I bit back a cuss that nearly flew out of my mouth, pasted on a smile reserved for negotiation meetings, and asked, "So, what's on your mind?"

Troy stuffed his hands in his pockets. "Me? Nothing. Just wondering if things were too rough. If you need help, don't be afraid to ask." His tone was mellow enough, but there was an asshole vibe to it.

My smile slipped a few degrees. What the fuck was that about? I composed myself and kept my voice even. "All good. Why?"

"No reason. If you need help, just ask," he said with the most innocent expression he could muster.

So he could tell Dad that he had been doing all my

work?

"Dude, your wife is pregnant. You need to see to her and not take on more work," I admonished.

"I can handle it. Just offering." He put his hands up in surrender, like he was harmless. *Yeah, right.* Knowing he found his mark, he stuck both hands in his pockets, smiled, then sauntered out the office.

My fists clenched, so I shook out the tension. Needing to get the fuck out of here before I did something stupid, I picked up my phone.

**Charlie Stevenson:** Don't think so. Thanks.
**Amberly Davidson:** Ok.

*Thanks,* screamed of assholery. I knew it and prayed she took the hint and gave up on me because seeing her had caused more problems than it was worth. Not to mention, I didn't want to have that fucked up breakup talk. So I avoided that shit like the plague.

**Charlie Stevenson:** Sorry it took so long to get back. Something shitty came up. But yeah, Babe, we can meet up. Lemme get home and change first.
**Shug Miller:** Ok. Where?
**Charlie Stevenson:** My place. We can have dinner together.

**Shug Miller:** What are we having?

**Charlie Stevenson:** Tell you what, how about you come over, and I'll take you to a restaurant?

The typing status flashed, then disappeared, and worry hit my gut.

**Shug Miller:** You mean like a date?

**Charlie Stevenson:** A friendly one, if you'd like.

**Shug Miller:** What does "friendly" mean?

**Charlie Stevenson:** Friends who go out to eat together. We can talk about your work.

**Shug Miller:** I guess

**Charlie Stevenson:** Is that a yes?

She took a second again. My feet fidgeted while waiting for her reply.

Unable to withstand the anticipation, I beat her to the punch.

**Charlie Stevenson:** Stop overthinking.

**Shug Miller:** Ok, then. Friends going out to a restaurant.

**Charlie Stevenson:** Cool. Come over to my place. Wear something fancy.

**Shug Miller:** You said that this was friendly.

**Charlie Stevenson:** Friends can go out to fancy places. Sometimes, I meet clients there.

**Shug Miller:** Tough life, corporate boy.

A boring life until this friendship made it enjoyable.

**Charlie Stevenson:** Don't knock it until you try it, corporate girl. ;)

**Shug Miller:** Touché, asshole.

A laugh burst out of me.

**Charlie Stevenson:** You just made a shitty day a lot better.

**Shug Miller:** Glad I could help. What time should I be at your place?

**Charlie Stevenson:** 6:30 good for you?

**Shug Miller:** Yessiree. ;)

# CHAPTER 16
## CAROL LYNNE

I arrived at Charlie's five minutes late and was freaked because of my tardiness. He answered the door wearing a white towel, his hair glistened with wet, and his well-developed chest and abs were on full display. Warmth filled his eyes, and a smile spread across his square face.

My heart went wild, and my mouth filled with saliva. I swallowed, affected a casual grin, and prayed my poker face persisted no matter what he threw at me. Reckon Charlie didn't realize his effect, which was a good thing.

"Sorry, Shug. Ran late at the office, finishing up an affidavit. Came home twenty minutes ago, so I hopped into the shower real quick." He stopped for a second, and his eyes traveled up and down my body. Goose-bumps trailed in the wake of his perusal. "You look good," he said, bringing a thumb to his lip while his gorgeous brown eyes examined me.

*Sweet baby Jesus. This man!*

"So do you," popped out of my mouth before I could stop it. Heat crawled up my neck while Charlie's grin grew wider into something naughty.

I covered with, "Sorry. Didn't mean to make that awkward. I'd been raised to mind my manners. It's almost a reflex to return a compliment." Hopefully, that didn't sound like babbling.

Charlie's eyebrows rose. "So, you don't think I look good?"

He goaded me.

Pursing my lips, I said, "Stop fishing for compliments. You know you do, and you know what they say about pride coming before the fall."

Charlie threw his head back, laughed, and side-stepped to allow me in. As I passed by, he slipped his arm around my waist and pulled me in close for a kiss on my head. His skin was damp and warm. He nuzzled my neck for a beat, pulled back, and said, "That hair-style suits you. You wear it up so often that I forgot how pretty and long it was. And what's that intoxicating perfume?" Charlie moved in again to my neck and inhaled.

My God, I nearly moaned. It felt so good.

My tongue flicked to wet my lips. "Um, thanks. And I'm not wearing perfume. It's a honey, vanilla bubble bath." I offered him a bright smile, which had his eyes roaming my face like he was trying to touch me with his gaze. It made me feel awkward and a little exposed.

"I'll get dressed. Have a seat and feel free to turn on the TV. The remotes are on the coffee table." His tone was soft.

I nodded and thanked him. He disappeared into his room while I walked over to the couch and sank into the cushion. Fishing the phone out of my bag, I scrolled through my emails and made notes on my to-do list.

Charlie's muffled voice sounded like he was on the phone. I fought the urge to listen and returned to my task.

Ten minutes later, he walked out of his room wearing a tailored monochrome black suit with a gray silk tie, his brown hair slicked back. He always looked hot, but this was different. He had a debonair quality, or as Momma said, he had his *fancy britches* on.

"You ready to go, Shug?" He asked with an arch of his brow.

I shot up from the couch. "Sure." My voice

sounded squeaky, and I cringed as I made my way to the door.

He grinned.

We walked from his apartment to his car with his arm around my waist. Throughout our ride, he kept putting his hands on my knee while we talked. No matter what he said earlier about this date being friendly, Charlie acted as though we were on a romantic one.

And I didn't know how to handle it.

Could I trust him? Should I? Or should I just enjoy this date and see where it leads? My head told me to keep my guard up, but my heart and body longed for him. This was always my dilemma regarding Charlie. I wanted him more than I should.

The host led us to cherry wood double doors after checking our jackets at the Cherry Crest Restaurant. When he opened them, my jaw dropped. Branches that intertwined ran along the ceiling. White cherry blossoms hung from them, forming a canopy. Beyond the branches was a glass ceiling where the stars were visible through their spaces. The chairs were a muted pink, cushioned velour. The table linens were crisp white, and an enormous stone fireplace sat in the center of the room. We were having supper in an enchanted forest.

I'd never seen anything so beautiful in my life, and it made my eyes well.

The host led us to a table for two by the far corner of the room. A burning tea candle, set in a crystal holder, spotlighted those near in an ethereal glow.

I struggled to suppress my sentimental emotions because this was too much to take in.

The host pulled a muted pink velour chair and waited for me to sit, then he placed our menus in front of us and left.

"What's wrong?" Charlie's forehead creased.

"It's —" I shook my head. "It's just so beautiful."

His worried features smoothed while his eyes and smile warmed. "Glad you like it, Sugar. I was relieved they were able to fit us in last minute. There was another place I had in mind, but you showed up looking enchanting. I wanted to take you somewhere that you would find equally so."

Charlie thought I looked enchanting? What could I possibly say to that? It was so sweet and unexpected. "Thank you." I hope he caught how heartfelt my sentiments were. His eyes roamed my face and stopped on my lips.

Fighting the allure to memorize the planes of his handsome face, I opened the menu and took a gander at the delicious items. "Do you feel like having an appetizer?"

He browsed his menu, and when the server showed, we ordered a charcuterie board and the house red.

"What was it like growing up with your sisters?" I asked.

Charlie's smile was a little tight. "My sisters didn't get along because Es emulated Bri. They weren't really rivals since Es was a few years younger, but she followed Bri everywhere. Personally, I think she was lost and needed guidance since our mother wasn't around." He picked up the crystal goblet filled with water and sipped. The light from the glass looked like a kaleidoscope reflected on his face. He put it down and asked, "What about you? What was it like living on a farm? Any interesting characters?"

I gulped water quickly and giggled as his words triggered a memory. He grinned in response.

"There was an older man—crazy as a coot. We called him Hillbilly Jack. He used to run out of his cabin, waving the white flag, which was his underwear. Luckily, he wasn't naked." I shivered at the thought.

Charlie chuckled. "Why did he do that?"

I shrugged. "Something about how he fought in the Civil War. I think he meant he participated in war reenactment and thought it was real. Told ya, crazy as a coot."

We laughed so much that the other patrons turned and stared. I can't remember the last time I had so much fun.

Dinner was amazing. The assortment of creamy cheeses, sweet grapes, and tangy olives was mouth-watering. I even ate a bit of salami, which impressed the heck out of Charlie. He thought it was a mark of me expanding my horizons.

After we finished our dinner, Charlie talked me into an espresso and dessert platter with a pastel assortment of petit fours and macaroons. The bite-sized confections were balanced with coffee. It was addictive, and I nearly finished the entire platter while Charlie sat back and smiled.

Charlie drove to the Brooklyn Heights Promenade after we left the restaurant. He wrapped an arm around my waist as we strolled past a man playing jazz on the saxophone. When I first moved here, it was shocking that people were as active at night as they were during the day. It was like they lived in shifts, so the city lights were always on.

Back in Mississippi, the night was night. No lights—pitch black except for the night sky. Sometimes I missed it, but over the years, I got used to New York.

We stopped by the rail and stared across the water at New York's famous, illuminated skyline that shone in the distance. "Do you think it'll be weird to move to another town?" I asked Charlie, who stood behind me, securing me in the warmth of his arms.

"Depends on how much you got used to this." He kissed the top of my head. "It could be a shock after you move. But, in your case, growing up on a farm, you may adapt faster than someone who didn't have your upbringing."

Hmm, never thought of it that way. Will it be boring out there? It wasn't boring on the farm because we had to fulfill our quota. Farm work took a long time, and then, of course, there was also school work heaped on to it, so I was plum tuckered most days.

"Why? Nervous about living alone?" His voice broke through my thoughts.

"Not really. Can't live too far away because I have to travel back at a moment's notice for work. I wondered what it would be like living in a town. Been a while, ya know?"

"Don't worry, you'll take to it like a duck to water in no time."

I shivered at the cool bite in the evening air, so Charlie decided we should leave.

The traffic light shone in the car as he drove. The soft leather seats warmed in no time, thawing my chill.

"What plans do you have for your garden?" Charlie glanced with a hint of a smile on his face.

"Carrots, zucchini, squash. Maybe onions. Definitely tomatoes. Things I can use to cook a stew." The load on my chest lifted as I ran down my list.

"You like to cook?" he asked.

"Wholesome cooking. Yessir." I nodded.

He smiled to himself and repeated, "Wholesome," under his breath.

Charlie pulled into a parking spot outside my building, turned off his engine, and asked, "Is it okay if I come up?"

Knowing exactly where this would lead, blaming it on my need for comfort, I smiled in answer.

# CHAPTER 17

While I opened the door to my apartment, Keith walked up the stairs with a girl and gave me a strange look before he minded his own business and walked past us.

After Charlie walked in behind me and closed the door, he demanded, "What the hell was that about?"

"Relax," I placated, "He thought I was a lesbian because he'd seen Sarah in here so many times."

Charlie's dumbfounded expression made me smile to myself, and his sudden burst of laughter startled me. "He thought you were with my sister?"

Giggle fits overtook, so I responded with a trite, "Yup."

"Jeez, that would've been weird." He said while wearing a goofy expression that made me giggle some more.

We walked over to the couch and sat down. Charlie wrapped his arm around my shoulders, and I rested my head on his rounded one, then ran my hand over the black, royal oxford shirt that molded to his broad chest. "Thank you for supper, it was beautiful."

Charlie's chuckle caused his broad chest to move under my hand. "No problem, Sugar. I enjoyed watching how much you enjoyed it." He ran his hands up and down my arms, causing goosebumps to rise. I shivered a little. "Cold?" he asked.

"Not really," I answered.

"What is it then?" His voice turned low, soft, and sexy.

"I like your touch. It makes me shiver." I admitted.

His laugh was a low, barely audible rumble.

"I love the way you feel, Shug. And the way you smell is addicting. You have a thing for scents, don't you?"

"Yes, but the non-perfume kind. The natural kind."

"So noted," he said in a voice that oozed honey, then continued to run his hands up and down.

Giving in to my need to stare at him, I drank in

every part of his handsome face. This face that I thought about more than I'd cared to admit.

Charlie's lips settled on mine, and he kissed me thoroughly, pulling at each lip. His mouth tasted like the coffee we had for dessert. When he broke away, it ignited a pang of loss that had me leaning in for more. Charlie kissed my jaw, trailing down to my neck, where he inhaled and moaned.

I ran my hand down his back, soaking in the power contained in its curves. Charlie fumbled to undo the buckles on my belt. I unsnapped it for him, then unwound it from my body and tossed it to the floor. My dress was a little complicated for him to figure out, so I undid the side knot, added it to the clothing pile, and stood there in my bra and thongs.

He looked me up and down, devouring me with hungry eyes.

"Bra," he said in a raspier-than-normal voice. I reached behind my back to unclasp it and tossed it on the growing heap. Then I stood and waited.

"Turn around."

I complied, and although I couldn't see him, his stare made my ass and lower lips tingle. A finger slipped between the seam of my backside, separating my thong from my skin, and a shiver ran down my body.

Charlie asked, "You okay, Shug?"

"No. I was...was just surprised." My whisper was raspy.

He pulled on the string, causing the fabric to stretch along my front. "Touch your knees," he commanded.

My hands traveled down to my knees—the material tugged to the side. I gasped as warmth slid across my folds.

Charlie's tongue burrowed through my flesh and flicked my clit. A moan escaped my lips, and I gyrated my booty against his tongue. There was fumbling behind me as he pulled on the thong and let it go, snapping the string back into place.

"Turn around," he commanded.

Facing Charlie's now shirtless state while he undid his pants, he dropped them along with his underwear and stepped out of them. He moved my arms up to wrap around his neck and hiked my legs around his waist.

He carried me to my bedroom, then released my legs one at a time. With his arms around my waist, he kissed each of my lips before kissing me full-on, tasting me like he was eating a ripe peach. The rumbling moan and warm cock pressed against my belly ignited a low-level hum that radiated to my sex.

Charlie broke our kiss and said, "Get down."

I pressed my frame against his muscled one as I sank to my knees, his body hair tickled along the way. I sat on my haunches, stuck my tongue out, and licked his cock from base to tip. Then I sheathed my teeth, fit my lips around his head, and slid him in as far back as he could go. My lips stretched and burned with the effort.

Charlie gasped, "Fuck."

I slid him in and out of my mouth, trying my best to contain my gag. Then, replacing my hand with my mouth, I jerked him off while my tongue played with his balls. He hiked me up from my armpits and tossed me on the bed. Before I knew it, he yanked off my thong, threw it to the side, and put his mouth on me. The sound of his tongue jiggling my clit filled the room.

He pulled away and said, "Sucking my cock turned you on? I can taste your excitement down here," then he flicked his tongue out, licking me.

I moaned and writhed. "Fuck me-please-I-need-you."

Charlie chuckled and ignored me as he kept up his torture.

"I'm gonna—"

He pulled away. "Don't you dare," Charlie warned with an edge in his tone.

"Please... I—" I moaned, trying to fight off the building tension.

Charlie moved up my body, lined his cock up with my entrance, and thrust deep, filling me till it stung.

I gasped and locked my legs around his waist. Needing to retreat from the twinge, I pulled my hips into the bed.

Something crossed that stopped him. After a moment, Charlie flexed slowly while he rotated his hips, building an ache that turned sensual by the second. Without warning, he thrust hard, making the headboard knock against the wall, and alternated between grinding and driving. I'd marvel at his control if I wasn't mad with a need that caused my fingers to claw his back.

I pressed my breast into his chest, needing to feel connection everywhere.

My hips rotated while his balls spanked my ass. The pressure built in my clit, causing it to pulse, begging for release.

He gave me all his weight, pushing me further into the bed, and moved hard and fast. Our panting and moaning echoed off the bedroom walls.

My body convulsed, and my vagina pulsed.

He powered into me a few more times, cried out, and shot his warm seed into me.

I held Charlie close while we caught our breaths. He moved over to the side a few moments later. Then he rolled out of bed, lumbered into the bathroom, and flipped the switch, casting the front of his solid body in light.

My eyes went straight to his thick cock. This man was a work of art. He winked at me, walked into the bathroom, and shut the door.

# CHAPTER 18

I blinked my eyes open at the filtered light through the slats of the pulled blind. A brief second of startle came from the weighty, sculpted arm draped across my belly. It tightened, rooting me to the spot as its owner's sleep-ladened eyes watched.

"Morning, Sunshine. How are you?" Charlie asked as his fingers traveled up from my waist, over my belly and my breasts, to my face, finally cupping my cheek.

*He stayed?*

I affected nonchalance, squinted my eyes, and croaked, "Good. You?" The memory of our enchanting night flooded my brain. Heaviness settled like a blanket on my chest and my mouth went dry as a bone. This is where he'll turn cold and make up an excuse to leave.

"Great, and not so good, but we can talk about it over coffee," Charlie answered.

I faced him, my brows pulled together. "What do you mean? You mad at me?" Better get this over with.

He frowned and his eyes narrowed. "Not at all. There is some stuff going down at work that will bleed into my personal life. That's why I wanted to talk over breakfast. I wanted to make sure you were good this morning before we got into heavy shit."

Considerate.

Heat crawled up my neck and guilt flooded my system.

I sighed, and in it was self-castigation. "Sorry. Okay, there's a spare toothbrush under the sink. You can use that."

"No need. I keep a gym bag in my trunk." He dragged himself out of bed and went to the living room. After the times we had sex, he made some excuse to leave as soon as we were done. I expected the same last night, but that wasn't the case. I bit my lip.

Charlie walked out of the front door in his crushed black pants and his black shirt untucked. I waited, eyeing the door from my bed, then squeezed my eyes shut as the familiar feelings of abandonment resurfaced.

The roiling in my gut over my impending depression peeved me off. To fight it, I kicked away the covers and scrambled into the bathroom, as though washing up might help.

Last night's workout ached my inner thighs and vag, reminding me of all that went on and how much I loved it. I only had myself to blame though, I know it and own it.

Images of that restaurant filled my mind as I brushed my teeth. I could've kicked myself for not snapping pictures. That kind of beauty needed to be committed to something more accurate than my memory. Then I would've had concrete evidence unmarred by the bitterness that'll eventually come, due to his abandonment.

Turning on the shower and testing its suitability on my palm, I stepped into the tub. Luxuriating in the warmth and surrounding steam was equivalent to a hug, at least in my opinion. Taking my time, I washed my hair, shaved, and cleaned myself.

Once done, I grabbed the towel that rested on the radiator, dried off, and twisted my hair in it. After considering my choices from the array of scented bottles, I selected the almond coconut lotion from the shelf over the toilet, squirted a dime-size amount in my palm, and rubbed it on my body.

The cool air gave me goosebumps as I walked into the bedroom. I yelped and froze.

Charlie sat on my bed wearing black basketball shorts and a gray tank. He reclined on his elbows, taking in my nakedness in the daylight. His eyes stopped at my breasts. "Cold?" He asked with a mischievous grin.

I shook my head with my hand over my heart to steady my breathing.

"I can smell you from here. Edible," he said. His eyes drank me in and it lit up my insides.

What the heck could I say to that? I held my head high while going to my dresser, then opened the top drawer and selected a pair of red lace boy shorts.

I tried to ignore the tingling sensation of his, probably filthy gaze, as I slipped each leg through my underwear and hiked them up.

A low moan, or heavy breathing, I couldn't tell, escaped his lips.

I opened the drawer underneath the top and hunted for the matching red lace bra. After finding it, pulling it out, and fixing it in place, I walked to my closet.

"Come here, baby," he commanded.

"In a second, I need to find some clothes," I said over my shoulder as I went to the closet.

"Baby, come here, or I'll throw you over my shoulder and give you the spanking you're asking for."

I rolled my eyes and walked over to his open arms. All of this tightened my throat because this was a side of Charlie I'd never seen, and I didn't know what to expect.

After I got settled, he buried his nose in my neck, inhaling, then found my eyes. "What's up, Sugar? Why the heavy mood?"

I shrugged, not able to articulate my feelings. "I'm sorry. I dwelt on stuff after you left, and it cattywamped my insides."

"What kind of *stuff* and...catty what?" he asked with a scrunched nose and humor on his lips.

I sighed. "Cattywamped. My version of cattywampus. Means...topsy-turvy. As for stuff. Nothing, really. Same old crap that gets me down when I think about it. I wasn't expecting you to return, so I got myself all worked up, and now I'm upset. You didn't do anything wrong, and I'm sorry I made you feel that way."

He kissed my neck and inhaled.

"I take it that you like that scent too?" I giggled at the tickle of his beard.

"I love every scent on you. Can't explain it, but I find it comforting. And it makes me horny."

My laugh burst out and I said, "I can tell," and wiggled my ass, earning his grunt.

"Haven't taken a shower yet," he said. "Care to join me?"

"Already took one, and I washed my hair."

He peppered small kisses on my chest, then slowed down his pace as he trailed them to my breast. His hand traveled up my lap and came to rest on my crotch, where he applied the slightest pressure and moved his thumb in a circle.

My breathing picked up, and I ground on his lap to match the rhythm of his thumb.

This would be so much better if I stripped. I got off his lap, reached behind to unhook my bra, and tossed it on the bed. Then I shimmied the boy shorts down my legs and tossed them atop the bra.

Charlie stood up and undressed, adding his discarded clothes to mine. Then he squatted, wrapped his arms around my torso and lifted me, causing my legs to automatically wrap around his waist. He secured his hands under my legs as he carried me to the bathroom.

Once there, I dropped one leg at a time to standing.

Charlie turned on the shower and placed his hand

inside. He stepped in first, then helped me in and leaned me back against the tiled wall. He bent down and took my nipple in his mouth, his warm tongue flicked it over and over, before switching to the other.

Then he kneeled in front of me, draped my left leg over his shoulder, and buried his face in my sex. His tongue lashed against my clit, stoking the flame. My hips jerked, and my feet flexed at how delicious it felt.

Charlie pulled away and stood up. He palmed my shoulders and spun me, so I faced the tiles. The tip of his smooth cock parted my folds, finding my entrance.

I stuck my ass out and he slid in deep.

I gasped.

Once fully sheathed, my muscles clamped around his familiar girth, and his hiss sounded in my ear.

He ran one hand down my body until his fingers pressured my clit, while the other moved to my breast. Then he thrust, bouncing me up and down on his steel rod.

My moan echoed off the tiles. This man awoke a savage need I never knew existed. So beautiful. So delicious. There was nothing more than this. I cried out against the mounting pressure that threatened to break. He drove me to the pinnacle so fast, with minimal effort, like magic from a dark sorcerer.

Charlie grunted, "So fucking hot." Then he increased his speed, pumping faster.

I lost it. My legs wobbled as the dam broke and energy flooded from my sex, causing a shudder to rack my body.

He growled as he powered hard into me three more times before he planted himself deeply.

We finished the rest of our shower, stepped out of the tub, and toweled off. Charlie left the room and headed to the bedroom, then came back carrying a small black pouch. He watched while schmearing shaving cream on his cheeks, and took a small razor to it.

I swiped my almond coconut lotion and reapplied it to my body.

"One of these days, you'll let me do that." He motioned with his chin to my lotion-filled palms.

*One of these days*. So this ain't a one-day thing. Everything in me lit up. Beamed...so bright.

A grin broke out, clearing my cloudy mood, and I teased, "You would be horny in a second if you did this. Then you'd want to sleep with me again."

He side-eyed me, tapped the excess cream off the razor, and said, "Sleep with you? I'd fuck that naughty little mouth of yours right now if my dick wasn't so damn sore."

I laughed despite being grateful soreness affected him too because I had sex back-to-back in…never.

Getting a grip, I pursed my lips. "Will your dick fall off?"

Charlie smirked, said nothing and washed up.

I laughed and walked out of the bathroom to hunt for some clothes.

Charlie followed me into the bedroom, went to his duffle and pulled out a pair of black athletic pants.

"Why do you carry a gym bag in your trunk?" As soon as the question left my mouth, I regretted it. I didn't want to know about his many conquests and how he needed something to change into.

"I play basketball with a few guys every Saturday morning. I keep a change of clothes and my toiletry bag with me at all times, so that I can shower afterwards."

I raised my brows while I tugged on my orange sweatpants, elasticized under my knees, and a white shell top. The landlord didn't turn on the heat in the building, so it was a tad nippy. "Saturday morning? Shouldn't you be there now?"

"I have somewhere better to be," he winked. "Besides, I texted them during your first shower to cancel."

My face melted in a smile. He smiled right back, his

dimples on full display. *This man.* This impossible, sweet, intense, man…with a magical dick. Hmm, Magic Dick Charlie, has a ring.

Charlie dressed in black track pants and a gray thermal Henley top hugged his broad chest.

"Stop staring at me like that, woman! If I fuck you again, my dick'll fall off, or did you forget?"

I laughed as he repeated my teasing. "We don't want that. But if it did, you might regrow one by magic."

His brows grew together and he ogled like I had two heads. "Nah, since we'll need it often."

Surprise hit my insides. "We will?"

Someone knocked at the door and I groaned at the interruption. With a smile on his lips, Charlie went to it, looked through the peephole, then he opened the door wide.

Sarah barreled through, pushing the twins in a stroller. She didn't even notice her brother stood behind her.

"I'd been calling you all night. You had me worried sick!"

"Sorry, I turned off my phone because I was on a date."

Her body jerked. "A date?"

"Yes, a date," Charlie answered as he let go of the door, and it swung shut.

Sarah pivoted to her brother, then looked at me with her mouth open and eyes rounded.

I laughed.

"How long have you two been seeing each other?" Her eyes bounced between us.

My laugh died down at her accusatory tone. We were adults who didn't need to explain ourselves to her.

Charlie answered, "If you must know, I took her out on a date last night."

He probably felt the same as I did, considering he just said, in a roundabout way, that it was none of her business.

"Charlie, she's my best friend. This is weird, especially since I didn't know that you had feelings for her," Sarah said.

*Feelings*. A strange word. I wasn't sure if he had any for me, and assuming he had wouldn't be to my benefit. For all I knew, he wanted to start a steady hook-up session. Maybe he felt lonely, and he just wanted company. Then again, he stayed last night, and that was something he'd never done before.

Shoot. We needed to hash things out.

Charlie softened his voice. "Look, Es. This is still a new

situation for both of us. I understand it may seem weird to you, but we need our space to figure things out. Okay?" Charlie went over to the babies and kissed their foreheads.

She stopped for a second after he put it in those terms.

"But you're welcome to stay and join us for breakfast." I jumped in before she assumed he was kicking her out.

Charlie had tossed me a frown for a moment, before refocusing on holding both of the babies' hands.

Sarah's face fell. "I'm sorry for dropping in." Charlie stood, and Sarah pushed the stroller towards the door. "I'll call next time. You two have a nice breakfast." She opened the door and expertly maneuvered the stroller out.

Once the door had closed, my hands clutched my hips and my eyes narrowed. "You had to say that? That was unseemly, and she didn't deserve it!"

He swiped under his nose. "I'll talk to her later. She can't drop into people's homes and demand shit. If we were seeing each other, then it's our business. She overstepped."

I swallowed at the conviction in his tone. He had a point on some level, and it took the wind out of my sail. We didn't have to report our relationship. Were we in one? Lordy be, I didn't even know.

"Speaking of which," I began, "We need to talk about our *relationship*. What are we doing? What's going on between us?"

"We're taking things slowly to see if we're a good fit," Charlie answered.

I didn't know how to feel about that. On one hand, I want to be with him. On the other, I didn't know if I could trust him. The long and short of it was, *Momma didn't raise no fool*.

"Slow, huh? Well… slow it is, I guess."

"You guess?" he asked with a touch of astonishment in his voice. I reckoned because he expected me to be overjoyed. Not me. I had more pride than that.

"I have reservations about relationships and I suspect you do too."

The crease in his forehead, the only tip-off to his feelings. I shrugged at him while he looked down.

"Yeah. Something like that," he admitted. A topic he didn't trust me enough to venture down. "You are more observant than I thought."

More observant than he thought? What the hell did that mean? He reckoned I was simple?

My face must have registered that I was fit to be tied because he hurried to say, "This is new for me too, Sugar. I'm still learning as I'm going and might mess up." He glanced down for a second, then met my eyes.

Charlie probably had a long list of casual hookups, but no real girlfriends. Maybe I should ask Sarah if there was anyone in his past. Hmm. Then again, possibly not, since she was weirded out that we were together.

"What are you thinking about so hard?" He interrupted my thoughts.

"Nothing. I was just wondering what we should do next."

"We should have breakfast, talk about the next show you're producing, and more about this dream house you want to buy."

"What about you?"

"What do you mean?" he asked.

"What's going on with you?"

"Nothing much to report with me. My life is the same old boring shit. It's not nearly as interesting as yours."

"I still want to hear about your *boring life*. You mentioned you wanted to talk about heavy stuff at work."

His gaze transformed into seriousness that stiffened my spine. Gathering me in his arms, Charlie kissed me. The sweetness of it warmed my heart. Then it dawned. Charlie used his body to convey emotions.

After we broke apart, I gazed into his warm brown

eyes, studying him. He did the same to me—gauging my emotions.

Charlie kissed the top of my head. "Thanks for looking out for me, baby. I love it like you have no idea. So, Shug, breakfast. Coffee and cronuts sound good?" he asked.

I couldn't hold back my grin if I tried.

# CHAPTER 19

I entered the lobby of Metro Hall with a bounce in my step after signing the contract that booked the venue when my phone beeped with a text notification. I knew who it was, and a glow erupted from my heart, school-girl as that sounded. A week had passed since we started seeing each other, and he'd texted throughout the day.

**Charlie Stevenson:** Busy tonight?

**Carol Lynne Miller:** No, Hunky Brewster. Have something in mind?

**Charlie Stevenson:** It's Friday. Wanna do something? And Hunky Brewster?

**Carol Lynne Miller:** Define "something." Getting busy?

**Carol Lynne Miller:** And I was addicted to the reruns while I was in college.

**Charlie Stevenson:** Haha. Love it when you cut to the chase. But I was suggesting along the lines of movies. Do you want to see anything?

**Carol Lynne Miller:** Never been to the movies. I'd just waited till they showed on TV, so I could watch them for free.

**Charlie Stevenson:** You're kidding, right?!

**Carol Lynne Miller:** Nope. Never been. Didn't have the money to go, and when I finally had, it wasn't something I had time for. Preoccupied with work.

**Charlie Stevenson:** Then that's what we'll do. I'll pick you up, and we'll stop at a burger place first for dinner. Then we'll go to the movies.

**Carol Lynne Miller:** A date?

**Charlie Stevenson:** Yeah. A date, Sugar. Pack a bag because you're sleeping over. As a matter of fact, keep your stuff at my place, so you don't have to lug a bag back and forth.

My stomach plummeted at his last line. Saying that was a massive step was an understatement, and I was unsure we should take it right now. We'd only been seeing each other for a week. How do I tell him without hurting his feelings? This relationship propelled me into uncharted territory.

Him too, probably.

**Charlie Stevenson:** Hello?

**Carol Lynne Miller:** Sorry. See you tonight. ;)

Hopefully, that was vague enough until I could figure out what to do. I pushed past the glass doors of the entrance and walked down the street towards the train station. Vehicular horns and squeaky brakes assaulted my ears immediately.

Then again, maybe I made a mountain out of a molehill. Folks left clothes at each other's places all the time. This would've been the kind of thing Sarah and I would hash out, but that was out of the question.

The situation with her was still a little weird since her awkward drop-in. Really though, I didn't under-stand why. My best guess was she probably felt betrayed. It would explain why she'd been too cautious over texts. I reckoned it was because she thought I'd report to her brother. I'd never do that, and it left me in poor spirits that she thought I would've.

These were things I never thought about when Charlie and I started seeing each other. I'd never thought about how weird it would be for Sarah, and how it would drive a wedge in our relationship.

My phone rang. A long string of familiar numbers from an unknown caller filled the display. Momma.

I swiped and lifted the phone to my ear, "Hello, Momma."

Breathing, and a click on the other end.

"Momma? You there?" I glanced at the screen, and it indicated the call had ended.

Hope my phone didn't drop the call. Maybe she'll call back. Nervousness coiled in my gut while I descended the staircase of the subway station.

* * *

That evening, Charlie waited in my doorway, smiling, wearing black jeans, and a gray thermal top with a black jacket. The shirt hugged his defined pecs, making him look delicious.

"Quit ogling me and get your jacket. You'll get your fill later tonight."

The back of my neck warmed, and I thanked my lucky stars he couldn't see it.

A naughty smile widened his lips and made his russet eyes glitter.

Wait. *Could* he see it?

I rushed to the closet for the jean jacket that matched my blue jeans and white t-shirt. I put it on and pulled my long hair out, so it settled down my back.

Charlie said, "Your hair looks beautiful when it's down."

I turned around to see him staring at my back. His eyes lifted to meet mine.

My lips quirked, and I said, "You sure let me know when we were in bed, and you grabbed it."

His smile morphed to a toothy grin. "A perk. With you, there are many, and I'll let you know later tonight. But come on, we gotta skedaddle," he said, borrowing my lingo. We were rubbing off on each other. Before you know it, I'll be waving my magical d–

Okay, not going there.

I grabbed the new canvas bag I bought on my way home earlier this morning. Small bottles of lotion, underwear, a nightie, and a toothbrush filled it.

We purchased movie tickets from the kiosk in the theater, then went next door to the burger joint and bought supper. There were no empty seats in the crowded restaurant. We ended up eating our burgers in Charlie's Lexus, which I preferred to the rukus of the fast-food place. The mouthwatering aroma of our food perfumed his car, which intensified its flavor.

I munched on my fries and asked, "What's the plan for tomorrow?"

Charlie supported his elbow on the door panel, while his hand gripped his burger. On the other hand, splayed the wrapper to catch crumbs.

Through his bite, he said, "Real estate agent. We're looking at houses."

I stopped chewing and gawked at him. The *we* part caught me off guard. "Are you coming to the viewing with me?"

He swallowed his bite and frowned, "Is that a problem?"

"No. No, it isn't. Just surprised you wanted to go. Reckoned it would've been the agent and me." I instantly regretted how shitty that came out, and I winced.

Charlie's face fell, and he asked, "You didn't think I wanted to go with you?"

Dang, my stupid mouth.

"It's not that. It's—" I searched my mind for the right words. "No one had ever looked after me. I've always been the one who took care of folks. Not used to anyone having my back."

He nodded, "Well, that explains it."

My brows elevated. "What?"

"Why you behave the way you do? You pull away whenever I offer help. At first, I thought you were too proud to accept it. But it's more because this is an unfamiliar situation for you."

It had more to do with being afraid of appearing weak. I hated pity with a passion. He was right about that. I had too much pride, and sometimes I let it impede making smart decisions.

"Something like that," I said, tossing him a lip quirk, unwrapped the foil of my plant-based burger and took a bite. As much as I didn't want to admit it, these fast-food places knew how to grill a burger. I closed my eyes and savored the burst of flavors that symphonied in my mouth.

Charlie chuckled, then said, "As a kid, my parents were always fighting, and so were my sisters. When I was old enough to help Dad at work, he explained that he sorted out fights businesses had with each other. I thought the world existed so that people could fight. Maybe they discovered who they truly were through that.

"The problem was that I didn't want to do it. I didn't want to fight. I just wanted peace, ya know? You could've figured it out through introspection and talking." He huffed, then continued, "I don't know. Maybe it only works for some and not others."

I swallowed my bite then said, "Look inside. See what you find and let your heart be your North Star."

The hamburger paused in its journey to his mouth, and Charlie's gaze roamed my face. "Yeah," he said in the softest tone. Something tender passed between us. Ties that bind.

We finished our meal and hurried into the movie theater. We scored two seats in the corner of the back row because the theater hadn't filled up yet. I sat by the wall, and Charlie sat on my right. He slipped an arm around my shoulder when they cut the lights for the previews.

We locked eyes, and his burned with intensity even in the dark. He moved in, and we pressed lips. Luckily, the booming sound of the movie disguised our lip-smacking and occasional moans.

Couldn't tell you what we watched. All I knew was I had my first make-out session at the movies at the age of twenty-seven with the sexiest man I'd ever met.

And it was *awesome*.

Later that evening, when we got to Charlie's apartment, he held my hand and led me straight to his bedroom. Tossing my canvas bag on the armchair at the far side of the room, he faced me and began stripping.

Sensing we'd begun our sensual play the moment he stepped in the bedroom, I sauntered over to the matching chair, and took off my jacket, followed by my t-shirt and jeans.

Charlie stood naked on the other side of the room. Gone was the playful, teasing man. In his place was one who possessed the gravitational force of the black hole.

In my red silk bra and G-string, I strolled over to him. When I got within touching distance, I veered past him to his bed. A low growl rumbled from the back of his throat.

I got on all fours and rested my head and hands down on the bed, offering my backside. The floorboards squeaked under Charlie's footsteps. His warm hands ran up and down my legs, his fingers caressing my folds on every pass. My body tingled and ached for more. I bit his sheets to stymie getting too worked up.

On the fourth round, his thumbs hooked into the straps of my G-string and tugged them down. I lifted my knees to help him slip it off.

Palming my chest, Charlie pulled me upright, then we kissed. I lost myself in the dance of his skillful tongue.

He moaned, then whispered, "You're a great kisser, baby."

The vibration of his voice worked its way through my body, and I clamped his lip between my teeth.

With the snap of his fingers, my bra came loose.

I took it off and tossed it on the ground.

Charlie crawled on the bed and laid back with his legs spread wide like an invitation. Cradling his head on an arm, he grabbed his cock with his free hand and stroked it. "Suck," he commanded, pronouncing the word with a sensuality that compelled me to wet my lips.

I made my way between his legs and stuck out my tongue. Running it from root to tip, I almost closed my mouth around him, when he gripped his shaft, preventing movement.

Charlie positioned the head on my tongue. "You want me?" he asked.

"Uh-huh," I did my best to answer.

"Then show me. Fuck me real good, with your mouth."

I guarded my teeth behind my lips. He removed his grip and I took him into my mouth as far back as I could manage. His hiss and moans filled the room. My eyes watered, and it took a few passes to get used to his size, but I didn't gag. Weirdly, I wanted to give myself a high-five for my accomplishment.

His arousal fed the growing ache between my legs, and I squeezed my sex in response.

Charlie hooked his hands under my arms, hauled me up his body, and rotated the both of us, so he loomed on top. The whole thing happened at blinding speed, so when he drove in his dick, I yelped.

He fucked at a relentless rate.

Locking my legs, I held on for dear life, my breath caught in my throat while he grunted like a wild animal. This. Only this. Only him and me and this gorgeous tortured I'd submit to any day. I ran my tongue along his salty shoulder, trying to bear against the building tension at my core.

His pace shifted to maddeningly slow, which hurled me closer to release. The deliciousness of it made me beg, "Please."

Charlie grunted and obliged by picking up his pace. He gyrated his hips, and I convulsed as waves of plea-sure shot through my body and curled my toes. I trembled.

He hissed through clenched teeth and stilled, spilling his warmth.

With a heaving chest, Charlie said, "Your magic mouth and tight pussy will be the death of me."

My lips widened and after a minute, he got up and disappeared into the en suite. The tap turned on, and the toilet flushed. He came out carrying a washcloth and gently cleaned between my legs.

This sweet gesture caught me off guard. Charlie had never done it before. Never looked after me, afterward.

It–

My God.

Searching his features in the dark, I found tenderness that did me in. Walls. Fear. Doubt. Came crashing down.

Charlie returned to the bathroom, the tap gushed then silenced, and he came out and climbed into bed. We positioned ourselves so that the front of my body lay on his. I nestled my head on his chest, my arm around his waist, and we drifted off.

# CHAPTER 20

Nicolette Peters, Charlie's real estate agent, stood on the sidewalk when we pulled up in front of the house. A tight-fitting, navy business suit hugged her tall frame. Her black hair was up in a well-constructed bun, and she was gussied up to pageant queen proportions in the makeup department.

Did real estate agents get this dressed up, or was it just her preference?

Charlie walked around the car, and she beamed when they shook hands. The smile froze on her face when I stepped out.

There was a slight drop in warmth, like she didn't

expect or want me there, but wanted to stay professional as we shook hands.

I pursed my lips and swallowed back a sigh. This was what I signed up for when I agreed to see this man regularly. Dealing with other women wasn't fun.

Even being a natural platinum blonde, I considered myself a plain Jane, and up 'til now, I'd been okay with it. Standing next to knockout Nicolette while she made eyes at my boyfriend was another matter. What do I say? How should I act? Should I even say anything, at all? Gah!

*Eye on the prize, Carol Lynne, eye on the prize.*

Shoving my feelings back, I took in the red-bricked, Victorian farmhouse with green trim that stood on a hill.

My word, what a heart-warming, dazzling prize it was!

I snapped a picture of the house from the curb. The opportunity to own it settled in. This splendor could be mine. All mine. Swear, I could've pirouetted, and thrown in an arabesque for good measure.

"This house is well within your budget, Carolyn. Plus, you'll have some extra for renovations."

"It's Carol Lynne—two names. And this house is gorgeous," I added to take the sting out of correcting her. We walked up the winding driveway. The house stood on a hill, like a beacon. It had a green porch, spindle posts, and a green roof.

"The previous owners had recently renovated, so you won't have to do much on that end. It's more about changing things to suit your aesthetic prefer- ences," she said as we walked up the driveway.

"Even better." I beamed, feeling like someone had flipped the switch in my soul.

"Wait until you see the inside. You'll love it," Nicol- lette said, stoking me in her salesy way.

I was too busy staring in awe at the house to see the meaningful glance Nicolette tossed Charlie and his returning wink.

After we gathered on the porch, she punched in the combination to the lockbox and took out the key, and unlocked the cream door.

Nicolette stepped in, held the door for us, and flipped on some lights. There was a flight of stairs that led to the second floor by the entrance. The white walls were contrasted with dark wood flooring and matching trim.

The living room's raised brick fireplace and bay window overlooking the front yard, had me imagining the holidays there. Christmas would be magical, dressed up country-like. And in the winters, I could read in front of a roaring fire.

My heart did a happy dance. I took out my phone and snapped a few pictures while the smile etched my face.

The hall led to a small, rustic kitchen with white cabinets, appliances, and green-tiled countertops. It was outdated, but it could be renovated a few years down the line. There was enough space to fit a small dining room table in the center in lieu of an island, so that was cool.

A back door in the kitchen corner led to a small deck and down to a decent-sized backyard with a rickety red garage. There was enough room to plant veg and install a fire pit. I'll probably need a lawnmower.

I entered *lawn mower* and *dining room table* on the to-do list app on my phone.

The four bedrooms upstairs were smallish and had dark wood trim around the doors and closets. The bonus was the en suite in the master.

Standing in front of the hazy bathroom mirror, I stared at my reflection, when Charlie's image joined mine. He leaned in and said, "You've been quiet. What are you thinking?"

"It's...perfect. It's everything I never knew I wanted." I said, and Charlie's eyes searched mine and his face brightened.

This was the Charlie I knew. This one. *My Charlie.*

Forgetting my awkwardness with her, I rushed to Nicolette, who stood by the bedroom window, and nearly bounced on my toes when I asked, "How soon can we put in an offer?"

With a triumphant smile, she said, "We can go back to my office and sign the papers to submit a formal proposal."

"Okay, let's do that," I beamed.

We walked out of the house and stood on the porch. I took the opportunity to inspect the neighborhood while Nicolette locked up. All the houses along the block were turn-of-the-century with well-maintained yards. Colorful patches of flowers dotted their fronts. It seemed quiet enough, definitely ain't what I was used to.

The sad, blue hydrangea by the sides of my porch steps...future porch steps, whatever, needed tending.

Nicolette's and Charlie's laugh snapped my attention. They were encapsulated in their little world.

My throat tightened at how he smiled at her. Eyes twinkling. The same one he gave me. Worse still was that she made eyes back at him. He'd itched to ask her out, I'd bet.

And maybe more.

Like he did with me.

At that moment, I knew one thing, last night meant more to me than it did to him!

My nose stung as I flung my attention to the house, to stave off impending tears. This house was a promise of something permanent and concrete. I wanted it with all of my heart—to own land. It wouldn't leave me for another. Wouldn't drop me like a hot potato.

It was real.

Permanent.

Everything I needed.

We drove to Nicolette's swank office on the Lower East Side of the city. I signed what felt like a million papers while my real estate agent glanced at Charlie all the while.

If my feelings were hurt, it was on me. But I'll tell you what, at least there was a bright side. When I move, we'll probably lose contact.

I thanked her for her help finding the property and shook her hand. Sick at heart, I walked to the door. "I'll wait in the car. Thanks again, Nicolette." My light tone sounded off, squeakier than normal.

"My pleasure." Nicolette's tone was civil enough, but I detected an undercurrent of *get lost* in her vibe.

And you know what? Happy to oblige.

I took refuge in the car. Desperate for a distraction, I replied to emails, and made a few phone calls to book vendors, while Charlie made his date, or whatever he was up to.

Charlie came out a few minutes later with his face set in stone, and slammed the car door extra hard when he got in. Although curious why he was madder than a puffed toad, I didn't ask, because his vibe warned that if I questioned him, he'd blow up.  He dropped me off at my apartment.

My thank you was met by his silence.

* * *

I was browsing for cheap lawn mowers on my laptop while gobbling down vegan chili casserole for lunch.

Pictures of the house filled my screen. Momma and I will be so happy there. Maybe she could work in the garden to grow veg, or take up a hobby. She could finally retire and be at peace without people giving her the stink eye.

The impatient knock on the door startled me at first. Then I rolled my eyes and dragged my feet to answer it, knowing who it was.

As soon as I got the door open, Charlie stormed past.

I closed the door in a stupor, followed him in, and

crossed my arms, waiting for him to kick-start his shit show.

"What the hell was that about?!" Charlie bellowed. He wore a jean shirt that molded nicely to his pecks. A different shirt from the one he wore this morning.

*Asshole.*

I fought past the shitty feeling in my heart and hated that I allowed him to make me feel this way.

Like I was disposable.

Like I was trash.

This was the last time I allowed anyone to make me feel that way. If this asshole was fixin' for a fight, he'd get one.

"What the hell are you talking about?" I asked, trying my damnedest to not shout back. A Herculean feat at this point, let me tell you. Because, what the hell did he expect? For me to be happy that he was getting laid by someone else? And quite frankly, how delusional was this bastard?

Charlie's expression turned nasty. His eyes glittered with it, and I knew... I just knew he was about to say something I'd never forgive. "You know, you'd think that you'd be grateful to Nicolette for doing a great job in finding your house. You'd think you wouldn't act like a stuck-up bitch."

My body seized, and jaw dropped as though he slapped me.

*Wow.*

Just...fucking...wow.

"That what you reckon? I'm a bitch, because I had a problem with you and her flirting with each other in front of me. I wasn't nice to your conquest, so that made me a bitch? You can get the hell out!" My arm flung out and pointed at the door.

Charlie didn't budge. He rested his hands on his hips and eyeballed me, with a scrunched face.

"What the fuck are you talking about?! I'd never slept with her. I represented her when she set up her company. There were some loose ends regarding severance pay from her previous job. That was how we met."

"That wasn't what was going on this morning. Her body language said that she clearly wanted more. And yours said that you were willing to oblige."

"My body language? I was trying to flirt, so she wouldn't fuck you over when making the deal. It was a negotiation tactic, Carol Lynne. I had my game face on."

"Then what about your clothes? Why did you change?"

"I played basketball with the guys and had a

shower after. It was a late game, considering I couldn't make it earlier, and Colin had something on as well. So we rescheduled."

"You're that committed to basketball?" What he said was nutty.

He relaxed his rigid pose, warmth returned to his demeanor, and a smile played on his lips. "Of course. And a word of warning. Don't bother me during the playoffs. I usually turn off my phone during games and will probably commit murder if I'm ever disturbed. This also applies to football, but especially during playoffs. I live for finals."

I jerked back at what he told me and what it meant.

He wasted no time enfolding me in his arms.

As soothing as it felt, I pulled away and double-checked. "So nothing happened?"

With a sentimental expression, he said, "No, baby. Nothing happened. Nothing will ever happen between me and anyone else because you enchanted me with your hippy ways." He leaned down and captured my lips. As his tongue coaxed and burrowed, my phone rang.

We broke apart, and I went over to the side table. Charlie followed, wrapped his arms around my waist, and put his nose to my neck while I answered.

"Carol Lynne." My stomach dropped at Momma's tone. It sounded like a ghost.

My body went rigid. "Momma? What's wrong?"

"They hurt me," she whimpered.

My brain froze, and a chill went down my spine. "Who hurt you?"

Charlie's arm jolted, and his body went rigid behind me.

"I don't know what to do. They hurt me so that I can't work and had reason to kick me out." Her voice was filled with panic.

"Stay there. I'm coming to pick you up. You're coming back here with me."

# CHAPTER 21

CHARLIE

We drove for two hours from the airport in Springfield to River Run Farms. Driving through the woods on a paved road, I finally understood the true meaning of backwater. It was the best way to describe the never-ending greenery. Thank God for GPS, or I would've definitely gotten lost, especially being pitch black outside. The only lighting came from our rental. This place gave new meaning to off-the-grid.

Carol Lynne's blue jeans, light blue t-shirt, and cowboy boots were a change from her usual flowing skirts and sandals. I figured since we were headed back to the commune, she would've dressed the part.

Carol Lynne's mood alternated between calm and

pensive once we boarded the plane. I itched to ask her about this place, but gave her extra time to process her feelings.

However, this situation made me seriously uncomfortable, given that there were so many unknowns at play.

What if her mother doesn't want to come back with us? We couldn't abduct her, and I had a feeling that Shug would be down for that. What if her mother overreacted, which caused Carol Lynne to do the same by dropping everything and coming here?

"Sugar, what's your mother's name?" We could start there, at least.

She snapped out of whatever churned in her mind. "Gladys Miller."

"How long has she been living on the commune?"

"Before I was born, she and my father ran away to the commune while she was pregnant with me. He took off after Lynette got pregnant with his daughter."

"Hmm," I huffed out loud without meaning to do it. Shug has a sister. Interesting.

Her mom, though. Whatever they ingrained might be too strong–

"What is it?" Her forehead creased.

"Well," I sighed, "She may not want to leave if she

has been living there for so long. Ever thought about that?"

"I know she won't, but we have to try. Besides, if they excommunicate her, then she won't have a choice anyway. Judging by that call, that was what happened," she said.

"Excommunicate? Shit, sounds harsh. While you were living there, had you seen it?"

Her eyes were fixed ahead. "Heard stories. They didn't really do it often."

"Who made these rules?"

"The founder. A guy named Chris Davenport. He died, so Lynette McGreevy took over."

My brows shot up. "What did he die of?"

"Don't know exactly. They'd announced he died in a car accident. Lynette took over soon after. All of it happened before I was born, so I could tell ya bits of gossip picked up over the years. I don't know the full story, but she runs the place now."

Weird. Super weird. "I thought the ideology was that it was community-run, and no one holds any sway over anyone else."

"Yes, that was what they told folks," she answered. "I mean in an ideal world, that was how it worked. But from what I know, the council holds all the power. It's their government.

"Pissed me off because they were all hypocrites, even being knee-high. But, as I'd gotten older and had seen how the world operated, I saw things differently. There will always be a ruling body in any group, whether it's a business organization or a group of people living together. No such thing as community-run."

She continued, "The problem was that folks who bought into it had no savings. When they are too old to contribute to the commune, they'll leave with nothing."

"Shit, that's harsh," I muttered.

She nodded. "Yessir. They wasted their lives, investing in something that should've been a temporary fix."

I wrinkled my brow, "A fix of what, exactly?"

"Food and shelter. The necessities," Shug answered with a shrug.

"Why can't they see this issue coming down the road? How has this been going on for so long, and what makes it so appealing?" I took a deep breath to slow my roll before I overwhelmed her, but damn it if this wasn't fascinating.

Shug shrugged, "Short-sighted? Folks who were desperate for work go there. They might have been homeless or had gotten close to it. River Run offered them a lifeline. They left once they got on their feet, and that was why there were always openings to live there."

"How was that different from a cult?"

Her pursed lips told me that I asked a foolish question, but I genuinely didn't know.

She sighed and answered, "As far as I know, it isn't. A cult has a central leader, and everyone is serving him."

What did she call what the founder did? None of this shit made any sense. I drummed my hand on the steering wheel and cranked up the AC. It was humid, even in October.

The voice from the GPS announced, "Arriving at your destination in ten meters."

Vigilant for the turnoff, I sat up straighter.

Carol Lynne did the same while her head moved around, taking in our surroundings.

I turned right and pulled onto a gravel path that led to a barn-style wooden building. Its windows glowed and the headlights from the rental shone on flowers that overflowed its window boxes.

I parked the car in a parking lot alongside a few other cars. Reaching over to place a hand on Carol Lynne's, I said, "If you want to leave, baby, let me know."

She placed her hand on mine, squeezed, then

unbuckled her seat belt and exited the car. Jogging around to meet Shug, who was already made it halfway up the path to the barn.

The wooden steps creaked under our weight. Carol Lynne pulled the paint-peeled screen door and stepped inside. A sitting area greeted us, and to the left was a reception desk. A clean-cut brunette sat behind it with her face illuminated by a computer screen. She looked up and smiled toothily at us.

"Hi, folks. Are y'all stayin' for supper?" she said in a heavy southern accent.

"No, thanks, we're here to see Gladys Miller." Shug cut to the chase. I appreciated her no-bullshit attitude.

The lady examined Carol Lynne for a second, then said, "I think she's in the back. I can get her for you."

Shug nodded and said, "Thank you."

The lady picked up the handset of an old phone and asked that Gladys come to the front. A moment later, a rotund, short woman came through the swinging door, clad in black pants and a clean, white chef's jacket. Her gray hair was in a low ponytail, and she wore a black newspaper boy hat–the same kind Reese wore when we met at Bri's wedding. What struck me the most was her droopy expression like she hadn't seen sleep in days.

When she caught sight of Carol Lynne, her face

transformed. "Sweet Pea," she shouted and rushed with renewed vigor to her daughter with her arms open for a hug. They hugged for a while.

Finally, Carol Lynne pulled back. "Momma, there's someone I want you to meet. This is Charlie Stevenson. He's my gentleman friend."

What the hell was a *gentleman friend*? I extended my hand for her to shake. "Hello, Ma'am, I'm Carol Lynne's boyfriend."

Her mouth dropped open as she gazed at me. "My," she whispered. Then, she shook her head like she was clearing it, shook my hand, and said, "Hello, I'm Gladys, Carol Lynne's Momma."

"Lovely to meet you, Ms. Miller." I extended my hand for a shake.

Gladys gawked at my hand, then snapped out of her stupor and shook it.

Her grip held firm. She seemed fine. There were no visible injuries as far as I could tell. So why did she tell Shug that she was hurt? I fought the urge to furrow my brow.

"Momma, what's goin' on?" Carol Lynne's southern accent deepened.

Gladys averted her eyes to her feet but not before I caught her grimace. "It was nothin', Sweet Pea. We worked it out not long after I called you." She glanced at the brunette, who sat at the hostess desk, staring at her screen.

Gladys returned her attention to us. "Are y'all hungry? We're about to shut down for the night, but I can fix y'all somethin' right quick."

Carol Lynne eyed me. We hadn't eaten for a while, so her hunger probably matched mine, but she still wanted my confirmation.

My sweet Sugar.

"Yes, Ma'am, if it's not too much trouble," I answered.

We followed Gladys through the dining room to a small two-seater by a window with wooden shutters. Overall, the lighting was subdued, probably because they were shutting down.

"Can't you join us, Momma? There's so much we need to talk about." The longing in Sugar's voice broke my heart.

"Not right now, Sweet Pea. Gotta fill my quota for this week. They're makin' me work overtime, so I need to get back." Her cheeks were flushed when she faced me. "Nice meeting you, Mr. Stevenson."

"You too, Ms. Miller." I smiled at her again. She gave a curt nod, then turned and left through the swinging kitchen door.

I took Shug's hand from across the table and

kissed her fingers. "You okay, baby?"

She shrugged, then leaned closer to me and lowered her voice to an almost whisper. "Was it me, or something didn't seem right?"

I leaned in to be closer because I plain old needed it. "It wasn't just you. She was evasive. After we eat, you talk to her while I find us somewhere to stay for the night. I can stick around for a few days before I have to get back. Phoned Dad while we were at the airport, and he assured me he'll shift my work to a junior for a couple of days."

She nodded and said, "That reminds me, I have to call Nicolette and tell her that I can't meet up in person anytime soon."

"Oh damn, I forgot about that," I said, nearly slapping my forehead.

"I haven't. My dreams are all tied into that house. I want it badly. Plus, I'm going to use it," she lowered her voice and leaned in, "To lure Momma away from this place."

I blew out a breath. "Let's hope it works. I have a feeling—"

A woman wearing black trousers, a crisp white shirt, and a bow tie, burst through the swinging door. Her brown hair was arranged in a sleek ponytail. "Hello, I'm Rachael, and I'll be your server tonight." She smiled politely and placed two menus in front of us. "What can I get y'all to drink?"

"Just water for me, thank you." Carol Lynne and Rachel looked over at me.

"I'll have the same, thank you," I said.

Rachael nodded. "I'll be back to take your orders."

Shug waited until the server walked past the swinging doors to ask, "What were you sayin' about not being able to get Momma out?"

"Why would she brush you off when you asked what was going on unless she didn't want to leave? Maybe she worked out her problem," I suggested.

Carol Lynne said, "My thinkin' was that it was too public of a place for such discussions. I can probably get more out of her when we're in private."

We both looked over at the brunette sitting at the reception desk.

"I don't know, Shug. That blush gave her away."

She giggled. "Are you some kind of body language expert?"

I dropped her hand and scowled. "I read people's body language for a living. It's a job requirement."

Her expression changed to contrition. "I'm sorry. Didn't mean anything by it." She pulled her hand back and hugged herself, leaning her elbows on the table.

My chest tightened and I wanted to kick myself.

She'd gone through a lot today, and I shouldn't have snapped at her. Needing to apologize, I moved my feet and hooked them around hers. Her smile was shy as she opened her menu.

I copied and asked, "What do you recommend?"

"Hmm, how about... the fried chicken, mash, corn, and a biscuit or chicken and dumplings? I haven't had chicken and dumplings in forever." Her voice held longing.

I grinned, "Then that's what we'll have."

When the server came back with our drinks, we placed our orders.

"So, has this place changed since you've lived here?" I asked.

"They added this restaurant a few years after I'd left for college. Momma talked about it all the time. Never seen it though."

My brows quirked. "Why were they forming businesses if they were against them?"

"They weren't against businesses. They were against the rat race and the lifestyle that the rat race supports," Shug explained.

"I guess that makes sense." I wrinkled my nose, and added, "A little."

Carol Lynne chuckled.

I smiled back, and the anxiety that had been sitting

# CHAPTER 22
## CAROL LYNNE

"Sweet pea, please don't do this. I got things worked out with Lynnette. You think I wanna stir up trouble?" Momma said in an agonized tone. Her face was etched in worry lines that broke my heart.

We were in her shanty. Everything was just as I remembered, except my bed was missing. In its place was a small, round coffee table and an old green armchair that Momma currently occupied.

Charlie stayed in the car to give us some time alone.

I shifted around on the squeaky mattress across from her, trying to find a spot where its springs won't poke me. Last year, she begged me to send her eight hundred dollars, so she could buy a new one. Didn't have the heart to ask what she did with the money.

"There won't be any trouble, Momma. This ain't jail. You ain't doing time. You're free to go and come as you please." I took out my phone, opened the photo gallery, and scrolled to the pictures of the house, then stretched my arm to hold it up for her. "This is the house I'm buying."

I swiped through the photos, explaining each to her. Her brown eyes, similar to mine, lit as she examined the screen. One of them was of Charlie, silhouetted by the bay window as he looked out at the front yard.

"He sure is somethin', Sweet Pea. How did you meet 'im?"

"Charlie is Sarah's brother. You remember Sarah? My friend who had twins." I scrolled through the library to find a picture of the fundraiser.

She examined the screen. "New York sure has handsome men. They look like movie stars."

I huffed, "Not all of 'em, I can guarantee that. There are some interesting-looking folks who ride the train. But there are plenty of movie-star men and pageant-queen women mixed in."

Momma took the phone, and to my surprise, swiped through the album like operating one was second nature to her. The expression on her face fell.

"Missed out on too much of your life, Sweet Pea." The disappointment that saturated her tone made my heart heavy.

"That's just it, Momma. You don't have to miss out anymore. We can live together. The basement is nearly done. After renovation, you could live there—rent-free, of course. I can see into getting your social security reinstated, and you can have your own life. You need to retire. You need to rest."

She shook her head as though she shook my offer out of it. "It ain't that simple, baby girl. I owe these people so much. Lynette took me in after your daddy left us."

My eyes narrowed, and I saw red. "That's what she'd told you? That you owed her? You worked all your life to earn your place here. You owe nothing!"

"Baby, you know it ain't that simple," she defaulted back to her go-to explanation. A line I no longer bought.

"You can't live here forever. You know that. If you come back with me, you'll have a place of your own and things to do. You can work part-time in one of the stores close to home if you want a job, but I think you should retire. We can find something for you to do during the day. You can work in your own garden and grow whatever you like. If you don't want to do that, we can find something else. Shoot, you can stay home all day and watch TV."

Momma averted her eyes, her expression pensive. She was fighting my offer, I could sense it.

I knew it would be a challenge, but I had no idea what I was up against. Coming here and expecting Momma to leave with us was naive. This place had been her home for so long that she couldn't up and leave.

I closed my eyes, allowing my body to slump as I reached behind to massage my neck. A migraine was setting in.

Maybe Charlie could talk to her. He could charm birds out of trees. If he used that silver tongue of his, she might listen.

One thing I'd learned was when I pushed Sarah too hard during the early days of our friendship, she stopped speaking to me. Couldn't have Momma do the same, so I'll need to back off.

Shoving down my wish to stay a tad longer, I asked, "Do you have any time off this week? We can go somewhere to talk some more. I can take you shopping to buy you some new clothes."

"No, don't do that. If you buy anything, they'll take it away from me because I ain't supposed to keep it. It belongs to everyone."

Fury shot through my system so quickly, I could taste it on my tongue.

I was going to FUCKING. KILL. LYNNETTE.

I swear.

Needing to leave before I did something I might regret, I shot up from the bed. Minding my tone, I said, "Momma, sorry, but I need to scoot. Charlie's waiting. He'd been lookin' for a place for us to stay for the night."

Hefting herself from the armchair, she said, "They kicked off the fall festival a few weeks ago, so there are more folks stayin' in town on the weekends."

That stopped me. "Fall festival? When did they start doing that?"

"A few years ago. We got new management workin' the front of the farm."

Some operation Lynette ran.

My face softened. "I promise, I'll be back tomorrow."

"Missed you, Sweet Pea," she croaked.

We hugged for a while because we missed each other.

After leaving Momma's, I strolled down a familiar shanty-lined path, knowing it so well that I didn't need my phone to light the way. The temptation to knock on the doors to check if the same folks lived there, took hold. But at this time of night, it would've been rude, and I didn't want to be a bother. Besides, these people needed their rest after working like a dog all day.

One thing that struck me was *the front*, as Momma called it, filled new buildings I'd never seen. Big ones at that, like she flaunted her more-than-likely tax evasion.

A funky odor hit my nose, distinctive enough to identify it came from animals. There was a petting zoo somewhere. One of the many additions.

Our rented blue sedan was the only car parked in the lot. Charlie slept reclined in the driver's seat.

I bit my lip as I opened the door and climbed in.

He opened his eyes and returned his seat to its upright position. "How did it go?" he croaked.

"Not well, but not so bad either. Truth is, I don't know. I thought once she saw the photos, maybe she'd want to leave with us. But it doesn't look like it."

"Did she outright refuse?" Charlie asked as he started the engine and tapped the button for the GPS. Then we pulled out of the parking lot and onto the dark road. The only illumination came from our car's headlights. The lined road and dogwood branches were visible about one hundred feet ahead—the rest faded to black.

"No, she contemplated the proposition, actually."

"Then I'd say you were a success. It won't be easy. Be prepared that we may walk away without her.

I gasped and tried to say something, but he cut me off.

"For now, Sugar. Doesn't mean we lost. It means we'll win later. What's important is laying the groundwork," he said.

"Where are we going?" I asked, ignoring his sobering words.

"To our cabin. I found one while you were talking to Gladys."

I exhaled and smiled crooked-like. Relief probably shone from my droopy face. At least we didn't have to sleep in the car.

We pulled up to a cabin Charlie rented for the weekend, situated among a cluster of cabins that were part of the campgrounds. I hadn't seen this place since my group of friends gathered here after the prom.

After he parked, he handed me the key card, then got our bags from the trunk.

I got out of the car, swiped the card, and flipped on the light switch. Wood paneled the walls, and a large bed took up a good third of the room.

Charlie wheeled our bags across the parquet floors. He pushed down the handles, laid them flat on the ground, and unzipped them.

"You take the bathroom first, Shug." He didn't have to say it twice. I could barely keep my eyes open.

Riffling through the tossed-about clothing in my luggage, I located a red shorts-cami set and the toiletry bag.

Brushing my teeth while in the shower to speed up the time spent in the bathroom, I toweled off, lotioned, and got dressed.

When I opened the bathroom door, Charlie stretched on the couch while the TV played infomercials.

I cut it off, gently shook him awake, and led him to bed. He'd done enough. Tomorrow was another day.

# CHAPTER 23

The following morning, after stocking up on more supplies at the store in the main cabin, we asked the gray-haired man at the front desk where we could have breakfast. He sent us to the restaurant on River Run.

I cut a piece of French toast and popped it in my mouth. A mixture of custard and maple syrup sheathed my tastebuds while I chewed on the pillowy bread. Savoring it, I shut my eyes and moaned.

The chuckle that came from Charlie jarred me out of my rapture. "That good, huh? I'd only seen you do that when I—"

I kicked him under the table to silence the dirty

thing he was about to say. He laughed, which snagged the attention of the other patrons.

After Charlie sobered, he asked, "Why do you think she had withheld Gladys's social security?" He asked as he cut his sausage, forked some eggs, and popped it into his mouth.

I shrugged, "That was how they ran things here. I told her about the house and how I could reno the basement, so she could live there rent-free, but she didn't want to come. The thing was, I had the impression she wished she could, and that bothered me. It's why I want to stay and keep fighting."

Charlie shook his head. "Had a feeling we were dealing with this."

My brows rose. "Dealing with what?"

"Battered Wife Syndrome."

My forehead creased, and I whispered, "She's not a battered wife."

Charlie explained, "Similar to that. She thinks she can make it better if she stays. You need to be prepared that she won't come back with us. But we can lay the groundwork so that she'll leave at a future date."

He said that last night and he was right, but I couldn't accept it. I didn't want to. She needed to leave. I shouldn't have waited so long to come back for her. I should've done it sooner.

Charlie lowered his fork and knife down and put his hand on mine. "Hey, it's going to be okay. This isn't the end."

* * *

We located Lynnette's office after the hostess of the restaurant made a quick call and hung up. She pointed to a small door on her right. The wooden stairs creaked under our weight as we ascended, but the sloped ceiling kept us from reaching the summit, so we stayed a few steps from the landing.

Lynnette was easy to spot. She stood by a window on the far side of the room, as tall and wiry, as I remembered. Her light brown, ratty hair hung to her shoulders, and wore dingy jeans and a sleeveless, brown plaid shirt–equally ratty, if you asked me.

In her dramatic way, she spoke without facing us. "I was wonderin' when you'd come to see me. Dropped in to see your Momma this mornin'. Had a little talk with her."

Lynette turned her head slowly to look over her shoulder. Her weathered face broke into a vile smile, revealing bluish stains on her teeth, I knew were there because of my memories. When I was a little girl, I figured she suffered from a lollipop addiction.

"Heard you asked her to move in with you." She waited for my response.

Already playing mind games. *Fucking great*. "Hello, Ms. Lynette," I said in a cool tone. "I'm buying a house. It has enough room, so I want Momma to move in with me."

Her brows rose, "To New York?"

"Yes, Ma'am. To the interior part, outside of the city."

She nodded, impressed. "Nice to see you're doin' well for yourself. You were a go-getter. You always wanted more. Glad to see you got it. This type of life ain't fit for everyone."

Nice backhanded compliment. I forgot her special talent. When someone called her out on her veiled insult, she'd play high and mighty. Typical Lynette. Why my mother pled loyalty to this woman was beyond me.

I didn't respond because she had the power to increase the misery in Momma's life.

Charlie piped up, "Is there anything outstanding that Gladys owes?"

Lynette's hard stare moved from me to Charlie. "She don't own nothin'. She ain't got a pot to piss in and can leave if she wants."

"Then why won't she?" I couldn't help the accusatory tone that seeped into my voice if I tried, because, who was she kidding?

Lynette's eyes swung back to me. "You'll have to ask her that, darlin'."

"I did and she won't give me a straight answer, so I'm askin' you."

Lynette pursed her lips and shook her head. "Don't know why."

She was lying. I felt it in my bones.

Dang! This was going nowhere.

I was a ping-pong ball bounced between Momma and Lynette.

Charlie spoke up, "So you wouldn't object to her leaving with us?"

"Course not. This ain't some hostage situation. Gladys is a grown woman and is free to come and go as she pleases."

But she didn't feel that way, and that was the problem. Why, though?

Charlie's smile, polite. "Good to know, Ms. McGreevy."

"Please call me Lynette, Charlie."

He bowed his head.

Something weird clawed at my gut and sent chills down my spine. How the hell did she know Charlie's name? He never introduced himself. If Charlie was shocked, he never showed it. Guess he must be in lawyer mode.

"We don't want to take up more of your time, Lynette. We'll be on our way." He wrapped his hand around my elbow and guided me down the staircase.

I didn't want to leave. I wanted to stay and question her till she gave me straight answers. But Charlie knew the ins and outs of interrogating people, and I had to trust him.

My manners kicked in. "Thanks for taking the time to talk to us," I raised my voice as we descended.

We made it down the stairs and out of the building. As we hustled to our rental, I glanced up at the window. Lynette stood there, watching as we left. Those contemptuous eyes I could feel through the hazy glass, zapped the hairs on the back of my neck.

Ice seeped into my bones, and a touch of hysteria had me swallowing as though that would make a difference as we climbed into the sedan.

After we pulled onto the main road, I asked, "What do—"

"Shhh!" Charlie cut me off.

My forehead creased.

He glanced over at me and placed his index finger to his lips in a shushing gesture.

Nodding, I moved my gaze out my window, needing to trust his lead again, even though it confused the hell out of me.

We pulled up to our cabin and got out of the car. Charlie marched around to my side, grabbed my elbow, and towed me in the brush.

My eyes rounded.

Whatever he was about to tell me, I didn't want to hear.

Charlie stopped, faced me, and drew me into an embrace. He ran his hands up and down my arms, then slipped one arm around my waist. The other hand massaged the back of my neck.

Weirdly, it had the opposite effect and my fear intensified, almost to the point of shaking.

He said, "She more than likely bugged the car and did the same to our cabin."

My mouth dropped open, and my brows shot up. "Heavens to Betsy! How?"

"She knew me. Knew my name. Knew that we were coming to see her, and she waited for us. She knew way too much for someone who we had never met."

"Why would she even do that?" I whispered, even though we were alone.

Charlie shrugged. "Don't know. I had a brain flash to Watergate when we first walked up to her office. She was alive back then. It might have been where she got her inspiration."

"Wait a minute. We're getting ahead of ourselves. That's one hell of a leap to take."

"The Feds do it all the time. After questioning that goes nowhere, they may bug cars. She probably bribed the innkeeper for help. She's keeping tabs on us."

I shook my head and asked, "Why would she go through all that trouble?"

He gazed into the distance and said, "Control. No. It's more. Fear. She's afraid of something. And you being here is upsetting the balance." He shut his eyes. "Shit. I'm gonna have to call Dad."

I couldn't keep track of all that he was saying. He didn't want to call Ray? "But if he could help, that would be a good thing, right?"

"Right," he bit out under his breath. Weirdly, I detected reluctance mixed with other not-so-good stuff.

"When we are in the car or the cabin, never talk about Lynette or your mother. Don't mention my father. Instead, talk about your house or the weather. That would be our safest bet."

*Safest*? Were we in danger? Icy dread crept up my spine because I already knew the answer to that question.

"Talk to Gladys about decorating your house when you're with her. For now, let go of convincing her she should come with you until I can think of what to do next."

Words were stuck in my throat, so I just nodded.

# CHAPTER 24

## CHARLIE

The next evening, I sat in the car and waited in the parking lot while Carol Lynne visited Gladys. I texted Dad in the meantime. Let's just say it went as well as *expected*. Sarcasm fully intended.

**Ray Stevenson:** What the hell is going on over there? One minute you're helping Carol Lynne. Next, you're telling me that her mother is being blackmailed.

**Charlie Stevenson:** I said, "seems," Dad. "Seems." I don't have all the facts, but it's the only thing that makes sense. The founder is holding something over Gladys's head. She's afraid to leave.

**Ray Stevenson:** Charlie, this isn't good.

**Charlie Stevenson:** I won't abandon Carol Lynne.

**Ray Stevenson:** That wasn't what I was suggesting. Try to convince Carol Lynne not to disrupt the situation until you have more info.

**Charlie Stevenson:** I sort of did that. She won't push her mom to leave, and that's the best I can do right now. I'll have to work on getting her out of here. It won't be easy because they miss each other.

**Ray Stevenson:** Okay.

**Ray Stevenson:** I'll reach out to my friend at the bureau.

**Ray Stevenson:** Be safe, son. Love you.

**Charlie Stevenson:** Love you too.


I took in his last line, shocked as shit.

My father hadn't said he loved me in a long time. I assumed he wasn't proud. Him being hyper-critical didn't help things either. Even sharing this current predicament battered the shit out of my pride. I wouldn't have done it if it wasn't an emergency.

Searching the barn at Lynette's office window, I found a distinctive female silhouette that stood like a sentinel since we'd been here. How the hell hadn't she given Shug nightmares, I'll never know. Lynette's weird mannerisms put me in mind of a fiend summoned from the pits of hell.

I cut my eyes to the looming trees for something less frightening to watch. Only by a margin. These trees added the creep show because they felt like ghosts.

And then there was the dark itself. In NYC, the lights were on every time of day. Didn't realize how much I detested the dark until coming here.

Not to mention those loud-ass crickets had fucked with my sleep and I hadn't gotten a decent night's rest.

I collapsed the seat and tried to get some shut-eye while waiting. Five minutes later, the car door opened, and my girl came in. I righted my seat, started the engine and tapped the display for the GPS. The clock on the dashboard read 11:45.

"How did it go, baby?" My voice sounded like I swallowed gravel.

"Fine. Better than last night. Filled her in on my life as a promoter. Bit my nails while doing it. You know what they're like around her, but she seemed interested."

Carol Lynne's cheerier vibe lightened my stress, but she shouldn't be talking about her mother just in case they bugged the car.

We pulled into the road and made it about a mile when headlights sped forward from the opposite direction.

Headlights careened at us.

I stomped on the gas, just missing a side-on hit.

Carol Lynne's scream rattled my brain, making me wince.

From the rearview mirror, the vehicle kept turning. Its screech filled my ears, and the crunch of metal hitting the tree jarred me.

I raced back to our cabin, on high alert, chest heaving. Pulling into our parking spot, I got out of the car, and went inside. Yanking on our suitcases, I opened them.

Snatching an empty plastic bag from Carol Lynne's case, I went into the bathroom and switched on the light. With my arm, I swept the bottle of lotion and my cologne from the vanity into the bag.

Carol Lynne rushed to the doorway, her hair messier than a moment ago, like she ran her fingers through it. "What are you doing? We can't leave now, just because we nearly got into an accident."

Was she kidding? "That wasn't an accident. We're leaving. That's that." The fact that she wanted to stay after what happened boggled the fucking mind. But I didn't have time to get into that now, because we seriously needed to hightail it the fuck out of this place first.

"It was an accident, Charlie. We survived. You're

blowing it out of proportion because you're tired." She placed her hands on my shoulder.

I stopped and gaped at her.

Carol Lynne asked, "How about this? Let's sleep on it tonight. If you feel the same way tomorrow morning, we can leave." She let that hang, then added, "We need a shower." Her blond head tilted suggestively.

I took a moment, flexing my jaw, debating her request while working to slow my breathing. Tossing the plastic bag on the counter, it slid into the sink.

At that, my woman's eyes smoldered, and she stripped, dropping her jeans and t-shirt in a pile on the bathroom floor.

I did the same while drinking in her nakedness. The glowing expectancy of those brown eyes of hers mesmerized me. For someone who had nearly been killed, she seemed weirdly in control. Another item added to the ever-growing laundry list of things I loved about her. This self-assured woman was tough as nails, yet feminine, sensual, and beautiful. Every element of her captivated me. Everything I wanted.

And it hit me.

I love her.

I loved her so fucking much.

When the hell did that happen, or had I always felt

that way? Would explain why I kept coming back no matter how hard I tried to forget her.

Desire for my Shug burned hot in the pit of my gut. She must have sensed the change in me because her eyes rounded and bounced around my face.

I backed her against the bathroom wall. Kissing her once on her lips, I trailed them down to her tits, then took her nipple in my mouth. I sucked and flicked each one with my tongue until she moaned. She tasted and smelled like dessert. *My sugar.*

Trailing lower, drinking in her scent along the way, until I reached the apex of her thighs. Without delay, my mouth latched onto her lips, and I licked up her seam. My tongue darted out at her clit, connecting to its home.

Carol Lynne gasped.

Her hips gyrated like she was begging to be fucked. I groaned against her pussy, loving her taste, not to mention riling her up made me so hard it was damned near painful. Her panting drove me wild.

I pulled away, wiping the trail from my mouth as I stood up, and shoved her to stand by the vanity, so we could see ourselves fucking in the mirror. I reached around to grab her pussy with one hand. Positioning my cock at her entrance, I thrust in until she was full of me, causing her breath to escape like a hiss.

Shug's walls gripped like a vise pulling the groan out of me, and my forehead slumped on her shoulder for a second, trying to not blow my load so damn fast.

Our eyes found each other in the mirror and I massaged her clit, giving her what she needed. Shug cried out, and I committed her expression, brimming with longing to my brain.

I hammered hard, shaking the sink with every thrust, and Shug matched my rhythm.

This woman. This bewitching woman owned me.

Shug's pussy clenched tighter, and I nearly came right then. Her legs shook.

I forced myself to slow down and growled, "Let go, baby."

Holding taut behind her, Shug bounced frantically on my cock, milking me and moaning all the while.

Her pussy throbbed, her juices warmed my cock, and she cried. Resuming movement, I thrust hard, over and over again until I lost control and shot into her.

Resting my forehead against her back, we fought to catch our breaths. After a while, I eased out, walked her over to the bathtub, and handled her like precious glass while we bathed.

Carol Lynne regarded me with confusion during our shower and dry-off.

While kneeling in front of her, I applied the coconut lotion all over her body.

When our eyes met, I said, "You are *mine*."

Her body went rigid. "Completely?"

My heart clenched. How could she not know how I felt?

"With all my heart," my tone ringing true.

Shug paled.

I didn't expect her to say anything back, so I stood up and led her to our bed. We got settled and while on my back, Shug stroked my stubbled chin, then bent her head and kissed me. Then she kissed a trail down my body and showed me how she felt with her mouth.

This woman. *My woman.*

# CHAPTER 25

CAROL LYNNE

My offer for the house was accepted this morning, and I wasted no time signing the papers through an e-signature program. Charlie and I celebrated in our special way, which involved him giving me a massage before things took a turn towards the erotic. We missed breakfast at the restaurant, so we drove further south for an hour to the nearest town.

After we chowed down on Angus burgers with fries and sweet tea at the local Roadside Burger chain, we hung out at the SuperMart for a little shopping therapy.

Charlie examined the tags of jeans on a rack. "Leaving has to be her decision. We can't drag her out of there or else she'll go back."

I sighed as I studied a white shirt. "I know. It's just that I have a weird feeling about that place? It ain't safe for her."

"Battered Wive's Syndrome is a powerful psychological relationship."

We'd been down this road more than once and it was understandable. At this point, not much to do except reassure her that she had me to count on, and a place to stay when she's ready to leave.

I was fighting an uphill battle, and it left me heavy-hearted and burned out. Our time here had been a roller coaster of emotions. The thing was, some part of me nagged she was still in danger, and I couldn't shake it. What kind of person would I be if I left my mother to face that alone?

"On the upside, think about how great it'll be when we get back, and you go on your final walk-through," Charlie said as he examined the jean rack for a replacement of his muddied ones.

"I suppose so, but I feel like we're doing wrong by leaving her here." My voice sounded pitiful. *Ugh!* I cringed.

"Trust me, Shug, you aren't. You can't force her to do something that she's not ready for. I'd seen it before. Look at Sarah. How many times did you try to get her to move on? It'll only work when she's willing.

"You fight for people and will do everything in your power to win those battles. That's one of the things I love about you, but you need to find a balance. Choose your battles." Charlie tossed a smile, then returned to the tags.

My heart lit up. *That was one of the things he loved about me?* My smile matched the radiance of my heart.

"I love you too." The words popped out of my mouth.

Charlie stopped his perusal and fixed his russet eyes on me. He blinked, searched my face, and said nothing.

The brightness that lit a few seconds ago faded. I inspected the shirt sleeve and studied the cuff as the back of my neck heated.

Charlie came closer. Still, I refused to look at him, so I pinned my eyes on the white button of the cuff like it was the most fascinating thing I'd ever seen.

Charlie's thumb lifted my chin to meet his intense gaze. The softness to his tone had steel behind it when he said, "I love you, Shug," and pressed a kiss to my lips.

As my heart melted, and it occurred that the first time a man told me he loved me was in the SuperMart. I giggled while our lips were connected.

We spent the rest of the time eating, stocking up on

travel essentials, and purchasing fun extras. I bought a few tops, and Charlie purchased a pair of dark blue jeans.

When we drove back to our cabin, Charlie grabbed our bags from the trunk while I opened the door.

And I saw it.

A bootprint on our ajar door.

The frame was broken where the latch plate had been mounted. I pushed it open and froze.

Our clothes were strewn about with the inner lining of pockets pulled out. The toiletries were scattered.

Charlie came up from behind. "What the fuck?!" he shouted and barreled past, shouldering me to the side.

I stood there, stunned, as he stormed into the bathroom, then walked out a second later and looked around the room.

"Was last night still a coincidence?" Charlie barked.

I blinked, and gawked at the shift in his mood.

He couldn't mean this was my fault, right? Maybe he did. And I guess he was right. This was my mom, so it was my problem. But he decided to come with me, dangit!

"Are you really going to do this, now?" My voice came out breathier than I would've liked and my eyes stung. "No one told you to come with me. That's why I do things by myself."

"You think I would've let you take off somewhere alone?" he shot back.

"Why not? I'd been alone all my life, I'm used to it!" I threw my arms out in a broad gesture, "This happens when people get involved." My eyes teared up despite my bravado. "Someone will always get hurt. Better it be just me."

Charlie gaped for a second, then his face fell. He came over and tried to gather me in his arms, but I pushed him away, struggling to free myself.

Didn't need this, or him.

He came at me again, and I pounded on his chest while traitorous tears ran down my face.

Charlie crushed my body against the large wall of his, while securing my arms until there was no more fight left in me.

Tired, my head dropped to his shoulder and I sobbed, hating myself for it. Hating this show of vulnerability. Hating that he could see my pain.

Charlie ran his hand up and down my back in a comforting motion, but all it did was make me cry harder.

"I hate her. I hate this!" I forced out through convulsing sobs.

"Who do you hate, baby?" he asked while his cheek rested against my head.

"Lynette," I answered when I could. "She always fucked things up for me. For Momma. I hate how much power she has and how much power Momma lets her have." With that, a fresh wave of tears started. All the feelings I'd worked to avoid hit like a ton of bricks.

Charlie's body flinched. He unwrapped his arms, grabbed my elbow, and towed me outside. I stopped crying, confused for a second until I figured out what he was doing.

We walked deeper into the woods as we had done yesterday. His room bugging theory made sense. I didn't doubt him. I could've written off last night as an accident, but not the break-in.

"It's a hunch," Charlie began, "But since we hadn't spoken about her in the car or cabin, she pushed us to divulge more info."

"Why would she want to do that?" That made no sense.

"She wants to know how much we know about her. My guess is she's blackmailing Gladys and wants to know if Gladys said anything about her, so she's going to push us to see how much we know. Then she'll decide what she wants to do with us."

I pinned him like a deer caught in headlights. My mouth and stomach dropped as I registered his words.

"We... we have to...the police. Call the police." My voice filled with panic.

"Soon, baby, but we need to set up ground rules first."

My eyes narrowed. What was he talking about?

He explained, "When the police get here, don't mention you suspect Lynette's involvment. The police are there for us to report what had happened for documentation purposes. We can't make suppositions. That's what lawyers are for."

I shook my head, "But you *are* a lawyer."

"In this circumstance, I'm not. I'm a guy who followed his girlfriend to see her mother."

Of all the things that could catch my attention, his use of the word *girlfriend* did.

He continued, "We need to play it smart. Luckily, our travel info and passports were in your handbag, so they didn't get anything important."

I sighed, "We're gonna need a vacation from all this stress."

Charlie smiled, "In due time, Shug. For now, think of your house when you feel down. Think about what color you want the walls painted. More importantly, think about how you'll be feeding me grapes as we lay on the couch in the evening."

That made me giggle despite my stress.

He grinned, his face relaxed from its tightness.

We walked back to the main building and spoke to the cabin owner. Shocked to hell that a crime went down on his property, he refunded our fee. At first, I thought that he'd been in on it. Now, I don't know.

We phoned the police, which didn't make the cabin owner jump for joy exactly, not that he seemed the type. In fact, he begged us not to, but Charlie, being Charlie insisted.

After the police took our statements and took pictures of our cabin in its strewn state, we packed our luggage. That evening, Charlie drove us to River Run so that I could say goodbye to Momma.

Then the horrible shit went down.

# CHAPTER 26

### CHARLIE

**Ray Stevenson:** Leave immediately!

**Charlie Stevenson:** We're doing that. She's visiting her mom one last time, then we'll drive back to the airport tonight.

**Charlie Stevenson:** Then we'll see what plane tickets we can buy.

**Ray Stevenson:** I'm gonna see what's taking Lauren Denato so long to get on this. I contacted her a few days ago.

**Charlie Stevenson:** Takes time, I guess. They can't rush into cases without scoping it out first. They aren't the police.

**Ray Stevenson:** This whole thing makes me crazy. My kids and the shit they get into.

**Ray Stevenson:** First it was Sarah, now it's you.

**Charlie Stevenson:** Carol Lynne was born into this situation dad, she didn't hook up with a psycho girl-friend like Reese.

**Ray Stevenson:** I know it's not her fault. But it's just that trouble has a way of finding you kids, even if you live clean.

**Charlie Stevenson:** Sorry, dad. Sorry bout everything.

**Ray Stevenson:** I know, son.

**Charlie Stevenson:** I better get going, see you when I get back.

**Ray Stevenson:** You do that. I love you.

**Charlie Stevenson:** Love you too, dad.

I squinted my eyes at the sudden brightness in the rearview mirror when a car pulled up next to mine in the parking lot.

A chill prickled my spine.

After the week we had, I expected anything to happen.

The driver and I locked eyes. He nodded curtly, then returned to his phone. His face, illuminated by its soft light.

My eyes drifted up to Lynette's office window. No silhouette of Lynette filled the space.

I fired a text to my woman.

**Charlie Stevenson:** Hurry. We need to leave ASAP.

**Carol Lynne Miller:** Alright. I need a minute. I'm helping Momma to pack.

My body froze for a second. I blew out a breath and typed.

**Charlie Stevenson:** She's coming with us?

**Carol Lynne Miller:** Yeah. When I showed up, she told me she wanted to get out of here.

**Charlie Stevenson:** Strange. But good.

**Charlie Stevenson:** Did she say why?

**Carol Lynne Miller:** No. I still don't understand, but right now, I don't care. At least she's leaving.

**Charlie Stevenson:** Will she be staying at your place?

**Carol Lynne Miller:** Of course.

**Carol Lynne Miller:** K. I gotta get back to her. Ttyl

**Charlie Stevenson:** Hurry!

The guy in the car next to me was still typing on his phone—no need to panic. Plenty of reasons why a random person pulled up beside me at this time of night.

I texted again.

**Charlie Stevenson:** Keep your phone on, so I can find your location.

**Carol Lynne Miller:** K

I hustled out from the car and kept the phone on to illuminate the way. Walking down a dirt path at night ranked up there with things I didn't want to do, but it beat being in the car like a sitting duck.

Locating Shug, I trudged into the darkness. The crunch of the ground underfoot, coupled with those loud-ass crickets, kept my company as I made my way to the shanty. Luckily, my fear of stepping in shit in the dark was unfounded. Surprisingly so, considering the potent odor of it filled my nose. Barnyard animals were close by, no doubt.

Barely knocking on the door, it tore open to reveal Carol Lynne with a harried expression. Beyond her, Gladys scooped contents from a drawer, then hurried over to a green, seventies-style suitcase and dumped her armload. She rushed across the room and repeated.

I stepped into the shanty and stood off to the side, so Carol Lynne could shut the door and resume helping her mother. She was right. Gladys behaved oddly, but questioning her motives wouldn't benefit us.

The shanty's bare walls made me sad. Devoid of

history, personality, any showing of joys or accomplish-ments. Jail, basically.

The curtainless window revealed the pitch-black night beyond its glass. What struck me the most was the splintered door trim beside me.

Did Carol Lynne grow up like this? Without privacy? *Holy shit.*

No wonder she left and never came back. Who'd want to live like that?

Gladys handed Carol Lynne a plastic bag and instructed, "Sweet pea, get my bathroom things and put 'em in here."

Carol Lynne took the bag and went to the bathroom.

We were too distracted to notice the shadow that passed by the window.

Seconds later, a crash exploded from the door, hitting the wall as it flew open and reverberated.

We froze.

Lynette rushed inside, past me, with her rifle pointed at Gladys. "Told you, you can't go! Told you the only way you're gonna is in a casket. Can't blame me for this, bitch!"

She pointed the gun at Carol Lynne. "Your meddlin' ass will be my first."

I lunged behind Lynette, wrapped my arm around

her neck, and yanked her off her feet.

She thrashed and her feet tried to find purchase but the speed at which I'd dragged her prevented it.

My heart drummed in my fucking ears, but terror propelled me onward. Squeezing the shit out of her windpipe, I hauled her flailing body onto the grass outside the shanty. The turf slowed my progress.

Lynette fired off a shot wild.

A scream and thump came from inside.

*Fuck!*

Her throat pulsed under my hand as she gasped for air. The wailing that came from within the cabin drowned out the sound of Lynette's gagging and wheezing. As soon as her body slumped, I let go.

God Almighty, what a fucking nightmare?!

I hustled back inside on noodle legs, and a weaker stomach after what I'd done, to find Carol Lynne by her mother's side. She pressed her hand to Gladys's upper arm while a stream of blood leaked down. As shitty as it sounded, I could've dropped to my knees and thanked God it wasn't Shug.

Gladys was awake and had a wide-eyed stare as she focused on the pool.

Hurrying to my girl, I held her in my arms in the most awkward embrace while she attended to her mother.

The other tenants gathered by the doorway.

A woman, who appeared to be in her sixties, dressed in a dingy blue bathrobe, came up to us. "Was wondering when Ms. Lynette woulda done something."

"Done what?" I asked while rocking my crying girlfriend. Couldn't tell if the trembling came from her or me.

"She was threatenin' her all the time, saying she was gonna do away with Gladys and there was no point to her life. Said she shoulda done it ever since after Davenport died."

My mind took off in a sprint, racing to put the pieces together.

*Holy shit.*

Gladys witnessed Lynette killing Davenport, and she'd been blackmailing her.

The EMT rushed into the room. I hadn't phoned them. Maybe another tenant had.

I pulled Shug away from her mother, to give the guys space to work.

"Clear out," an EMT ordered the onlookers.

They filed out, glancing at Gladys as they did.

"There's also a body outside," I said to the technicians. "I left her lying in the grass. She was the one who came in and shot her."

One of them got up and left. He came back in and

asked, "Where?"

"Back in a minute, baby." I massaged Shug's arms, then let her go.

Going to where I left Lynette, the EMT handed me his flashlight. I took it and shone the light on the grass, around the vacant spot.

"I didn't make it far with her," I told the EMT who searched with me. "Heard screaming coming from inside the shanty, so as soon as Lynette gave up the fight, I let her go and went back inside."

"If she got up and is still hurt, she could probably make it to the hospital," he said before taking back his flashlight and rejoining his fellow technician.

I took my phone out of my pocket, activated the flashlight feature, and did some investigation as they wheeled Gladys on a stretcher into the ambulance.

One local, an older guy, came up to me. "Found her yet?"

"No." Fear and relief roiled in my gut. She couldn't have gotten far. Thank God I didn't kill her.

"Don't surprise me one bit it came to this. Ms. Lynette was mean to folks, but real mean to Ms. Gladys," a gray-haired guy said.

"Is that why there's a high turnover in this place? I mean, is that why everyone keeps leaving?" I reiterated.

"Yes Sir. How you gonna treat people mean and expect them to live on pennies? Don't work."

"Was that why you had to expand the farm into other businesses rather than the nut butter one?" I asked.

"Suppose so, don't know. Ms. Lynette kept to herself. She don't do much to help in the field like she used to. Got more money now."

I shook my head. Not only had she violated not-for-profit laws, but labor laws as well. Utter bullshit, wrapped in a high-and-mighty belief system.

Carol Lynne came over to me after the ambulance drove away. "We should go to the hospital. They gave me this before they left." She extended a business card with the hospital's name, address, and some phone numbers.

I took the card and slipped it into my back pocket. "Let's finish packing her things, Shug. Gladys won't set another foot in this place once she gets out of the hospital." I said.

Shug buried her face between my pecs, and her body shook. I ran my hands up and down her back until she calmed. The tenants who were gathered around the shanty eventually cleared.

We went back inside to finish packing, lugged the suitcase into the trunk of our rental. Soon after, the

# CHAPTER 27
CAROL LYNNE

Every time a nurse passed by, I wanted to hound them for news about Momma.

Charlie took a seat next to me and held two paper cups of coffee. He placed one on the ground, then peeled back the seal on the lid and handed it to me.

I accepted it with gratitude, appreciating its warmth that seeped through my clammy fingers.

"Thanks," I said with a grateful smile.

His brown eyes were soft when they bounced around my face. He picked up his cup. "Let me know if you get hungry, so I can buy you something to eat."

"Thank you." My sullen tone matched my dismal emotions.

Charlie's face fell. "What's on your mind, Sugar?"

I rubbed my forehead and sighed like a tired husky. "Thinking 'bout Momma. How she hadn't said anything about any of this. I didn't know it was this bad, or else I would've picked her up a long time ago. Would've brought the police with me. Something."

The failure that gnawed on my heart was amplified by the voices in my head. And you know what? I deserved it.

Charlie placed a hand on the back of my neck and massaged.

I leaned in and closed my eyes, letting his hands loosen the tension.

Charlie glanced around and lowered his voice. "Glad you didn't, Shug. No way you could have fought with that woman. You don't know how relieved I am to be here because what could've happened, didn't."

My heart melted, and the reassurance of his words spread through my body faster than the coffee would have done. My smile was closed-mouthed, and I rested my head on his shoulder. This man saved my life.

He wrapped an arm around me, pulled me closer, pressed a kiss on my head, and rested his cheek there.

A doctor wearing scrubs came through the double doors and called out, "Miller."

Charlie and I rose and walked past the double door

he held open. A chorus of beeps from machines in the examining rooms echoed while we walked to the far end of the hall.

"The bullet grazed her arm, luckily no bones were broken. She's in x-ray right now for a final check. All things considered, she's lucky."

I pressed a palm to my heart, and expelled a breath. Charlie placed his hands on my shoulder and massaged. "Thank you. When can we see her?" I asked.

"After we're done with the x-ray, an orderly will come out to get you."

"Thanks again," I said to the doctor. He gave a head nod and directed us back to the waiting room.

Charlie was on his phone sending a text. He'd been doing that since we got here. Whoever it was, their conversation didn't make him happy, based on how he ground his jaw afterward.

Momma was discharged an hour later. She hobbled to the car and didn't say much while Charlie drove us to the airport.

# CHAPTER 28

"What's that noise?" Momma asked when a closing door echoed from outside. Unfamiliar sounds still took some getting used to, even after it had been a few weeks since she moved in with me.

"Keith from across the hall," I answered while researching an e-signature program.

Charlie had been inundated with work since we got back, so we hadn't seen much of each other.

Additionally, Momma had trouble with being left alone. I missed Charlie and would've loved to spend some nights over at his apartment, but living in fear for so long had taken its toll on her. That meant I took her with me wherever I went. At this rate, she'll probably need therapy.

Later that evening, Ray and Charlie showed up at the apartment to pick us up for the final walkthrough.

Ray had been civil to both of us but cooler to me than he used to be. Can't say it didn't tweak my heart. I understood why but was hurt all the same. At least he'd managed to charm Momma, so that was a load off.

Nicolette waited for us on the sidewalk in her curve-hugging blue jeans and white angora sweater. My sloven white t-shirt, worn jeans with a brown belt, and moss green, cable knit cardigan, hammered at my confidence.

Charlie must have sensed it because he'd slipped his arm around my waist after we'd entered the house and had never let go, despite Nicolette's attempts to get his attention.

Bless him.

"How long have you been working in real estate?" Ray asked my agent.

"About four years," she answered with professional politeness.

I bet Ray thought she would be a better match for his son, seeing as there was nothing dangerous about her or her family.

Okay. That was a shitty thought and unfair to Ray. But the bitter part of my brain told me he wanted that.

Momma, Nicolette, and I passed through a door in the kitchen that led down to the basement.

I said to Nicolette, "I was telling Momma that we could renovate, so she'd have all this to herself."

"Oh yes. The previous owners hooked up the plumbing and gas line since they used it as a rec room. All it needs is a coat of paint, curtains on the windows, and you're ready to go."

Momma's eyes lit up when she mentioned curtains.

Hugging myself, I frowned at my feet. She lived without her dignity for too long. I wrapped an arm around her shoulder, wishing that I could go back in time to take her out of that place sooner.

"Is it just you two that will live here alone?" Nicolette asked me and Momma.

*Woah.* Forward much?

I swallowed that bitter taste this woman left me with because I didn't want to screw up this deal.

"Hopefully, she'll make some room for me too," Charlie answered as he walked down the basement stairs with his dad following behind.

I beamed at him and my body sang. "Of course," I said.

Charlie came to me, slipped his arm around my waist, and kissed the top of my head.

Ray's face turned to granite. It made me feel weird as though he seriously disapproved of our relationship.

I returned my attention to Nicolette.

In a cool tone, she said, "When you get your lawyer, send them my number so I can forward the paperwork."

My smile, achieved with effort. "I'll get on it."

Charlie spoke up. "I could help with that. I know a firm that deals with real estate law—"

"If it's the same one I think you're referring to, then check if they're available. I spoke with Allan the other day, and he said that they were up to their ears in case-load," Ray interjected.

I slouched.

"I'll call them tomorrow to touch base." Charlie ignored his father.

I jumped in before this got out of hand. "I could find someone. It's no trouble. I've errands to run tomorrow, anyway."

"See? She can handle it," Ray said to Charlie.

Charlie's eyes narrowed, and his jaw flexed as he stared at his father. "I said I'll look into it." His tone held an edge.

I chewed on my lip as the tension between them

grew. There's something there. More than just Ray's disapproval of me.

Nicolette's overly bright tone was directed at Momma. "Carol Lynne told me that you have an interest in gardening. Want to see the outside?"

I seized the opportunity to leave with them. We climbed the stairs and went out through the backdoor in the kitchen. Momma scanned the area around as though she searched for something. Thankfully, no one noticed, or if they did, they didn't ask.

Fishing out the phone from my cardigan pocket, I added a call to my HMO on my agenda tomorrow. The quicker Momma visited a therapist, the better.

# CHAPTER 29

"Just a second," I called out as I ran to answer the door after having just refilled the candy bowl.

Navigating the maze of stacked boxes scattered around the living room made me feel like a mouse. But I didn't have time to unpack as quickly as I would've liked, due to work frenzy.

I opened the door to a group of kids dressed as ghosts, fairies, and superheroes.

They chorused, "Trick-or-treat."

I complimented each child on their costume and dropped candy into their pillowcases.

A lady that held a baby dressed in a pumpkin

costume glanced behind me and asked, "Did you just move in?"

"Yes, a week ago, with my mom. It has been a whirlwind of unpacking."

She laughed good-natured. "I bet. Welcome to the neighborhood. We have a ton of kids here. My husband is manning our door while I'm out."

"In my old building, we didn't have trick-or-treaters, so this is new," I added out of politeness.

She nodded and smiled. "This neighborhood is different from the city. More like a small town. Great for kids."

After her group ran off to the next house, she wished me a Happy Halloween and left to follow them.

I waved, shut the door, and went to sit next to Momma on the couch in the living room. She erupted in a laugh at her new favorite sitcom on TV. Since we'd moved, she had taken to the television. If we weren't out, she was in front of the TV. I didn't mind since she never had it, and she was fascinated.

"Ya know, Sweet Pea, if I knew what I was missin', I woulda left a long time ago."

"Yes, Ma'am." Ha! The devil is a liar! She was too scared to move, so I didn't take that comment to heart.

My feet fidgeted for a bit, and I cleared my throat, wanting to broach something on my mind since we moved, but didn't have the guts. "What do you think about having folks over for Thanksgiving?"

Momma's forehead creased, and her guard came up. "Who you fixin' to invite?"

"Charlie, of course. Sarah, Reese, their babies. Maybe even Ray and Connie." I threw the last one in, though I was unsure if he'd accept.

"I don't know. Too many people," she said.

Momma was getting comfortable with Charlie since she saw him the most. She didn't like Ray after the last time we saw him during the walkthrough. His harping on Charlie frightened her.

My head tilted sympathetically. "I understand how you feel, but these are folks I see most of the time, and over the years they treated me like family. I just wanted to do something nice for them, since they'd been more than generous to me."

She sighed. "All right. If they did a good turn for you, then I suppose it would be right. Besides, good deeds are the work of *His* hands."

"Thanks." My smile hurt my face. I kissed her on the cheek, to give her the affection she'd seldom received most of her life, just as the doorbell rang.

Grabbing the candy bowl, I got up to answer it. Charlie stood there, carrying a messenger bag that hung at his side. He'd slept over most nights. I wanted to ask him to move in with us but needed to discuss it with Momma first. I doubted she would approve since we weren't married.

Charlie planted a soft kiss on my lips and smiled. His eyes twinkled when he pulled away. "Hey, Shug."

My lips tingled, and my insides turned to mush while taking in my hot man's stubbled square jaw. The faint woodsy scent of the cologne he bought during our shopping trip back in Mississippi, still clung. I wanted to paste myself to him and take a larger whiff, and I probably would've if it wasn't weird.

But knowing Charlie, he would've cracked up, delighted in how much I couldn't resist him.

I snapped out of my trance and stepped aside.

As Charlie passed, he winked, sending the butter-flies wild in my stomach. He slipped out of his loafers, and hung his tailored, black pea coat in the closet. Then he went over to the couch and kissed Momma's cheek. "How are ya, Gladys?"

"Keepin' on. Forgot how busy this holiday can get. Poor Sweet Pea hasn't had a moment's rest."

"Did you get dressed up when you were a kid to celebrate Halloween?" Charlie asked my mother as he settled in the armchair he'd donated to us from his bedroom back in the city.

I rested the candy bowl on the coffee table and settled on the couch near Charlie.

"We couldn't jump over a nickel to save a dime," she waved dismissively. "All we could afford was painting our faces. Momma sent us trick-or-treating cause it brought in free food, and we had fun doin' it besides. But not like the kids today with them fancy costumes."

"You had other kids around?" Charlie asked.

"Yessir. Two sisters and a little brother." Sadness colored her tone.

"What happened to them?" Charlie asked as he lifted his laptop from his bag and placed it on the side table.

A shadow crossed her face. "They died when they came to visit me on River Run."

Charlie's froze, and his eyes widened as he fastened them to my mother.

Momma continued, "She didn't want them to get to me. So a car accident befell them."

Charlie's alarmed eyes met mine, asked a silent question.

I nodded in silent confirmation.

"You must've had a tough day. We should get supper on the table," I said in desperation for a change of subject.

"I'll warm it," Momma said as she hefted herself off the couch and went to the kitchen. She insisted on cooking. I told her she didn't have to, but she felt obligated since she lived here for free. Not to mention, she didn't like my vegetarian cooking because it wasn't slathered in lard.

"How was your day?" Charlie asked.

I smiled at his sweetness. "Fine. Contacting bands for their rider sheets. Same old, same old. How about you?"

Charlie sighed, and his expression sagged, "Had one of those days I wondered why I was doing this job. Dad had been on my case lately, giving me a hard time, nitpicking everything I did. Feels like I don't have room to breathe."

Bet he was pissed 'cause his son hitched his wagon to what he considered the wrong horse. Maybe Ray and I needed a pow wow to settle our differences before this gets out of hand. "I'm sorry, sweetheart. Is there anything I can do? Maybe I should talk to him."

"Nah. Been on my mind for a while about striking out on my own. Look at how it has worked for you?" he gestured to the living room.

Things were that bad between them? *Dang*. "I work in a different field, sweetheart. It'll be different for a new lawyer. You'll also have to figure out if you want to start over at this point in your life."

His face fell. "So you're saying I shouldn't do it?"

The disappointment in his tone made me feel lower than a bow-legged caterpillar for discouraging him.

"Not at all. It's a great idea if that's what you want. It's just that you need to weigh a few factors before deciding. Research where you're going to find cases now that you don't have Ray's company to rely on. Research getting another office set up and where you want to do that."

"Do you need a lawyer?" A charming smile played across his lips, and I succumbed because I couldn't fight it–not that I should anyway.

"Not at the moment," I answered while hopping onto his lap. Charlie folded me into his embrace and Lordy be, did it feel good.

"Supper's ready," Momma called from the kitchen just as we'd melded our lips, earning my groan and Charlie's chuckle.

I climbed off and adjusted my clothes, while my man did the same. We held hands and went into the kitchen.

Judging by the late hour, there won't be more trick-or-treaters. We could eat without interruptions–great because hangry didn't look good on me.

While we dished chicken casserole onto our plates, I said, "I want to host Thanksgiving dinner. What do you reckon?"

Charlie nodded contemplatively. "Sounds nice. Who are you planning to invite?"

"Sarah, Reese, their kids, of course. Ray and Connie. Bri and Troy."

"So, my family?" he asked with a smile.

"Yes," I quirked the side of my mouth.

"I'll invite them," Charlie offered.

"I'll call Sarah. If she doesn't receive an invitation from me specifically, she'll be pissed. You can ask your dad and Bri," I said.

The doorbell rang. Momma froze with bugged eyes and her spoon halfway to her mouth.

Charlie got up. "You sit and eat. I'll be right back."

Momma's expression didn't change.

My heart picked up its pace, and icy dread made the hairs on the back of my neck stand on end. Shame seeped in for letting Charlie face something alone. I rose and scooted around the table to join him.

"Wait," Momma called after me, but there was no way I'd leave Charlie.

He opened the door to teenagers dressed as the devil and Pocahontas. "Trick-or-treat," they called out.

My heart returned to its normal pace, and I let go of the breath trapped in my lungs. I smiled, swiped the candy bowl on the coffee table, then handed it to Char-

lie. He dropped treats in their pillowcases and comple-
mented their costumes.

Seriously, I needed to see Momma's therapist
because my paranoia made me unhinged.

# CHAPTER 30

Charlie manned the door while I cooked dinner with the ladies. The men congregated around the TV, watching the football game while debating plays.

I was in the kitchen cooking our Thanksgiving meal with Momma and Sarah. Her twins were at the ankle-biter stage and were getting into everything.

Ray, Connie, Bri, and Troy showed up at the same time. They probably had driven here together.

Sarah and Reese brought over charcoal lemonade, which seemed to be their favorite because they always had it on hand.

Connie and Ray brought a vegetable platter. Bri and Troy brought a purchased pumpkin pie and a few cans of whipped cream. Luckily, I baked apple and pecan pies last night, so we had variety.

The aroma of mac and cheese and stuffing filled the air when Bri opened the oven door. She had just passed her first trimester, where the aversion to the smell of food was at its strongest. "No turkey?"

Momma set down a ceramic dish of fried butter beans on the table. "Downstairs. We're using my oven to bake it."

Connie, whose shoulder-length blond hair stood out against her elegant black sweater with a golden necklace and blue jeans, asked, "You got the basement all fixed up?"

"Yes, Ma'am. They finished two weeks ago." My mother answered with a pleased tone.

"Great. May we see it?" Connie's enthusiasm and sweetness won the war against my mother's guarded nature.

Momma opened the basement door. "Sure, we're goin' downstairs. Y'all hold down the fort." She flipped the light switch, then led Connie and Bri in the basement.

After they left, Sarah asked, "How is she handling everything?"

"Better since she has been seeing a therapist. Charlie had gotten her social security straightened out, so she has been receiving income. She bought a new couch and bed. Next month she's planning on buying a TV. She uses mine at the moment. I'll surprise her for Christmas by taking her on a shopping trip to replace her worn-out clothes that needed replacing years ago."

Sarah's eyes rounded. "Wow, sounds like a lot on your plate. Is she good at being alone? The last time we spoke, you told me you had to take her everywhere you went."

"The therapist said that part of her anxiety comes from not being busy. It's like a muscle that she needs to build over time," I explained.

"You'd think that when a person escapes an abusive situation, they'd relish every freedom," she said.

"They will, but it takes time, especially after how long she stayed."

Sarah tilted her head and asked, "How are you doing? It must stress the hell out of you to deal with all this and work at the same time."

Seriously, I loved Sarah. Even when she'd been lost in her abyss of pain a few years back, she had always been sensitive to others around her.

"Things at work are going well. But all my carefully laid plans usually get shot to hell during the day of the gig. My runner, Ben, deals with that stuff. Right now,

I'm in promotion mode to boost ticket sales, so I've been using social media a lot."

The oven timer on the stove beeped. A minute later, the faint bing came from the one in the basement. The scent of the delicious food got to us, so we scrambled to set the table and carve the turkey. There were so many of us that we used the kitchen table as a buffet and ate in the living room instead.

A warm glow ran through my body. I'd never felt this level of comfort before, like everything was right in my world.

Parking on the bench by the bay window, I fed the high chair-bound twins so Sarah and Reese could enjoy their supper.

A prickly sensation ran down my spine, and the hairs on the back of my neck stood up. I took a gander behind me, out the window, scanning the front yard and houses beyond.

An empty street, save for the maroon car pulling into our neighbor's driveway. When the door opened, I recognized the neighbor's daughter who climbed out of the driver's side.

When I turned back, my eyes collided with Charlie's. His glittering russet eyes were filled with warmth as he chewed on his bite, while the surrounding men focused on the game.

My returning smile held shyness because Charlie stirred my yearning, and my cheeks heated as a result. I refocused on feeding the babies with a stomach full of butterflies.

# CHAPTER 31

December came with *challenges*. That was how I chose to regard it. The basement reno took more money than anticipated, so I ran low on cash. This meant I took small odd jobs in PR for extra funds.

Momma still didn't want to be left alone while I met with vendors in the city. I ended up carting her along, equipped her with a clipboard, and introduced her as my assistant to explain her presence.

"When will the food be delivered?" I was staring at the calendar on my phone while Ben checked his.

We were on our second allotted walk-through of the venue.

"Scheduled for two hours before the event starts."

He answered while scrolling through the dates on his phone. "By the way, we are missing two rider sheets for two of the acts."

"Which ones? I'll contact their managers," I asked.

He scrolled through the list on his screen. "McRiff and Savage Lyric."

I typed notes on my spreadsheet under the outstanding rider section and added them to my call sheet.

Mom glanced around with suspicious eyes and a scrunched forehead. A permanent expression while we were out. I hated it but tried to be patient because this must be weird for her. Living on a farm for so long then dropped into the epicenter of the corporate world, they taught us to hate, must've been all kinds of weird.

One of the many things I was worried about was how well she'd take to living in New York. She looked around a lot like she was searching for someone whenever we drove into the city. The car horns, squeaky brakes of trucks and buses made her cringe, and pedestrians shouting at one another made her jump.

She was suspicious of Ben when they'd first met. Although I didn't tell the other managers about her past, I texted him about it because we met regularly.

Ben proved himself cool, though. When they'd first met, he complimented her and told her how she reminded him of his mom. Then he took a photo of her from his wallet and showed it. She immediately warmed up to him.

"Okay, thanks for the update. We'll meet closer to the event, but text should something immediate come up."

He agreed, and we said our goodbyes.

On our way home from Metro Hall, we stopped at Fresh Food Mart grocery store to buy a can of butter beans for supper. While we were in the bakery aisle, Momma stopped "What is it?" I paused filling a small paper bag with freshly made bagels from the bin.

"Lynette's here."

*This again.* I rolled my eyes. "If Lynette was here, don't you think she would've already made contact? It had been a few months since you moved."

"She always waits for the right time to do things. She plots," Momma explained.

"She has too many things that will take up her time back at the farm. She won't have the time to come all the way up here," I said in hope that logic would calm her.

My phone beeped with an incoming text. Pulling it out of my pocket, I glanced at the screen.

**Charlie Stevenson:** On my way. Leaving work now.

**Carol Lynne Miller:** At Fresh Foods with M. Will be

home soon.

We paid at the checkout. After loading up the trunk with our cloth bags full of more groceries than we intended to buy, we drove home.

"Will you be okay to stay by yourself the night of the show, or do you need to come with me?"

I pulled into the driveway and parked in the garage. We got out of the car, and I popped the trunk. Momma and I grabbed the bags from the back.

"Don't know, Sweet Pea. We'll have to see. Things are going okay at the sessions, but my skin keeps crawlin'."

I reached up and slammed the trunk closed, then pressed the button on the keypad to close the garage door. "You'll get used to it. I'm worried about you being around all that noise if you go to the concert."

After inserting the key into the back door lock, I tried to open it, but it wouldn't budge.

"What's the matter?" Momma asked.

"Door's stuck. Come on, let's go through the front," I said. We walked to the front of the house and opened the door, then hauled in the bags. The aroma of coffee hit as soon as we walked in.

Shoot! I forgot to unplug the coffee maker. There will probably be a mess on the counter.

Placing the bags on the ground, we took off our boots and coats and put them in the closet. Then we grabbed the bags and brought them into the kitchen.

"Wonderin' when you bitches would show."

I jerked, dropped the bags, and whipped to the side.

Lynette leaned against the counter, sipping from our teal-colored mug with the picture of a Buddha on the front. The rifle sat near her on the counter.

My feet nearly gave out as I bolted to the back door and tried to open it, but it wouldn't budge.

She put the coffee cup on the counter. "Don't bother. I closed every exit point. Left one open for after I do what I gotta do."

"Get out!" Momma shrieked like a wounded animal. That wretched sound branded itself in my memory, and I'd go to her if I hadn't been too scared to move.

Lynette focused on me. A nasty smile curved her thin lips, revealing messed-up teeth beyond. "Your Momma agreed to be my prisoner when I tried to kill her the first time after she threatened to rat out that I killed Davenport. Hell, she even named you after me and gave up your daddy."

My jaw dropped as I glanced at my mother. My entire childhood made sickening sense.

Momma was stone-faced.  Her eyes fastened on

the intruder.

Lynette continued, "I own everything about her, even you. And you had the *fucking nerve* to walk into my home and demand she leaves! Like hell, you're takin' what's mine!"

# CHAPTER 32
## CHARLIE

I hoped the drive to Carol Lynne's would've calmed me because my day had been total shit. Squinting and bitching while hammering on the steering wheel didn't help, but fuck, I needed to hit something.

I was shutting down the office when Amberly showed up and demanded to know why I was ignoring her.

For fuck's sake! Even while we were fucking, we waited until after the workday was over. And where the hell did she come off harassing me about a hookup? She crossed the fucking line! I shouldn't have gotten involved with her in the first place. I know that now.

After that, Dad stormed into my office and bitched

at me for shitting where I ate, then told me that Amberly quit, and it was my fault. I admitted that Amberly and I saw each other for a while but stopped since I'd been dating Carol Lynne.

*Swear*. I have to get the fuck out of that company. Can't deal with Dad and the weird-ass looks from Troy. So tonight, I'll research what it'll take to set up my own practice.

As I pulled into Carol Lynne's driveway, the front door was left wide open.

*Weird*.

Maybe they were still unloading the groceries.

The rickety garage door was down.

Hairs on the back of my neck stood up. I got out of the car and closed the door. As I approached the house, muffled shouting and crying came from inside. Carol Lynne and Gladys got along, so…what the fuck?

I climbed the porch steps with heavy legs of lead.

Zeroing in hard on inside the house, I missed the other car pulling into the driveway.

"Shoulda killed you while I had the chance when you yapped about going to the police. You liked Davenport so much, you could join 'im." The voice had the same drawl as Gladys' but the wrong tone.

Footsteps shuffled, and Carol Lynne screeched, "Wait, wait!"

I froze in the doorway.

Hatchet-faced, Lynette rushed at me with a familiar-looking rifle. "You." She aimed and drew closer. Suddenly, her eyes widened at something behind me. She aimed at it and fired.

*Fuck!*

A thump shook the ground and rattled the door.

I spun around.

My father sprawled on the porch with a gunshot wound on his forehead as blood ran out of it and pooled beneath him.

I wailed and sank to his side. His glasses cracked from the fall, and his eyes were still open behind the shards.

A blast exploded inside the house, and I jumped. Lynette dropped like a sack of potatoes.

Gladys's shaking hands aimed a handgun at Lynette's body.

Carol Lynne's face, awash with horror, rushed over to me with tears in her eyes, her hand extended.

My hands trembled as I lifted my father's glasses and ran my palm down his eyes, closing them.

Carol Lynne dropped beside me and held me as I shuddered in her arms.

My howls were so loud that I barely registered when someone shouted, "Call nine-one-one."

# CHAPTER 33

CAROL LYNNE

Not that much later, police cruisers and an ambulance arrived.

A few other officers ran past us with their guns drawn and went into the house. "Ma'am, put the gun on the ground and your hands up in the air," one of them shouted.

*Shit!*

She must've complied because they said, "Now back away from the gun."

That familiar pull to defend her, hammered at me, to talk to them and clear her name. But there was no way I'd leave Charlie, who sobbed and trembled in my arms.

I rubbed his back, hoping to ease his pain in any way possible.

An officer commanded, "Turn around and put your hands behind your head."

I stretched my neck to see inside, but I couldn't see past the backs of the two officers who blocked my view.

One of them wrenched his handcuffs from his belt and advanced on her. Seconds later, they'd frog-marched her out of the house towards the police cruiser and shoved her inside. A female officer fastened her seat belt and got into the front.

Momma's pleading eyes haunted mine through the window as the cruiser drove away. No doubt, they'll revisit my dreams like everything on this horrible day. In a gesture of reassurance, I held out my hand to her.

"Wait, she's innocent," I pleaded to the officer who stood closest to me.

"Ma'am," the officer began. "Can you tell me what happened here?"

I answered, "My mother and I just came home from the grocery store when that lady was already in here, waiting for us."

"Where did she wait?" he asked.

"In the kitchen. We tried to run out when we realized she was there, but we couldn't open the back door. She told us that she sealed every exit." My stomach felt weak, and I wanted to throw up.

The officer stopped writing and asked, "What's his involvement?" He pointed to Charlie with his pen.

"This is my boyfriend, Charlie Stevenson. He came in while we were being held up. She saw when he pulled up to the house, left us, and went to him."

"Sir, can you tell me what happened?" the officer asked.

Charlie passed a palm under his nose and took a deep breath.

I gave him an extra squeeze for reassurance.

"Her eyes went wide, she aimed the gun behind me and shot," Charlie answered with such forced control that it killed me.

He went on, "Then there was another shot, a second after, and she dropped to the ground."

The officer stopped writing. "So she shot this man," he pointed at Ray with his pen, "and your mother shot her?" He pointed at Lynette.

I nodded and said, "Yes."

The officer said, "You two need to stand to the side while we take pictures of the scene."

I helped Charlie up and led him down the driveway to the curb. We stood by the cruiser.

Another cruiser pulled up, and an officer in a white

shirt got out and walked to the porch. The other officers came out of the house and talked to him.

I hugged my body and shivered because my blue button-down jean shirt didn't stand a chance against the December weather. Charlie's pea coat had suddenly settled around my shoulders. Dressed in a cream sweater, black trousers, and a black scarf, he could withstand the frosty temperature.

"Thank you," I whispered.

Charlie glanced down at me and gave a quick nod but said nothing. A rock formed in my gut at his reaction. *He just lost his father, cut him some slack.*

It was just past dusk. Two ambulances and the cruiser's flashing lights had illuminated our street. The lights were on inside my house as the officers roamed through.

One officer questioned the neighbors who gathered on the sidewalk. The suspicious way they looked over at us reminded me of how the people on the farm regarded Momma and me—of how we were pariahs in that community.

My dream home was now a crime scene. This house was supposed to bring joy and warmth. Now it'll be remembered for the murders that took place here.

An officer waved at the ambulances. The EMT officers got out of their vehicles, brought out a stretcher from the back, covered Ray's body with a white blanket, and then loaded him onto a stretcher. Charlie turned away while they handled his dad.

Minutes later, they did the same with Lynette.

*God.* Poor Charlie. He lost his father because of the mess in my family. I bit my lip.

An officer put yellow tape across my front door.

Warm tears ran down my face. Covering my mouth with my palm, I wept as silently as I could manage while misery ate me up.

Charlie's hand rested on the back of my neck.

I moved in and buried my face in his large shoulder, and he folded me in a hug.

# CHAPTER 34

The interrogation room's dingy white walls needed a fresh coat of paint years ago. The frosted windows didn't allow visibility to the outside, though it would be impossible at this time of night.

I stared at the mirrored glass opposite from where I sat, hugging myself. They had taken Charlie somewhere else. I hadn't seen him since they brought us in. My worry, questions and paranoia floated in my mind, unchecked.

The one thing that bugged me was the gun Momma carried with her. Where did she get it? Did she carry it with her all this time?

For some reason, my brain flashed to the lumpy

mattress, and I froze.

The money she begged me for. How did I miss it when I'd helped her pack back at the cabin? She must have slipped it in the bag when she sent me to fetch her clothes from the closet.

I shut my eyes and massaged my temple. Momma saved our lives. If it wasn't for that gun, we would've all been dead by now. I took a steadying breath and did my best to calm down.

After about a half-hour of waiting, a tall, rounded man lumbered into the room from a door beside the mirrored glass. His white shirt had green pit stains, and his belly hung over his belted brown slacks.

"Evening, Ms. Miller. I'm Detective Russel Madigan. I read the report and am sorry we have to meet under these circumstances." He came over to the table, rested a file folder, and took the seat across from me.

"Can you tell me how my mother is doing?"

"We have her in holding. We'll question you and Mr. Stevenson for the preliminaries. If everything checks out, you can take her home. Mind you, this will take a few days, so she won't leave tonight."

My mouth dropped. A few days! *Shit!*

Madigan's sharp brown eyes moved over my face. "Sorry, we can't wrap this up sooner. We need to be thorough, and these things take time."

"I understand. It's just... I'm protective of my mother, and my boyfriend just lost his father." In the back of my mind, it occurred to me that I should guard my words.  But then again, judging from all the law shows I watched, guilty people guarded their words.

"Let's start with the basics." Madigan opened the folder and his eyes scanned his notes. His salt and pepper comb-over didn't hide his glistening scalp from the fluorescent lights. He readjusted his glasses and sniffed to clear his nose.

"When did you move into your current residence?"

"October twenty-fifth."

Madigan pulled out his phone and tapped away. Then he jotted something down on the paper while murmuring, "A Sunday." He glanced up and asked, "What do you do for a living?"

"I'm a concert promoter. I work in the city."

"How long have you worked this job?" He asked, reading from the file.

"Not long. I've been doing it part-time until recently. Last summer was the first concert. I'd just produced another concert a few months ago."

"What about your relationship with Mr. Stevenson? How long have you been seeing him?"

Tough one. I don't know when we made it official. "We've been serious for about three months."

He stopped taking notes and asked something that wasn't any of his business because it didn't really pertain to the case. "What do you mean by that?"

My face heated and I cleared my throat. "He's my best friend's brother. We've known each other for a while and have hooked up a few times. But we've been seeing each other exclusively for about three months."

His brows rose a notch, then he continued writing.

I hugged my torso and hunched.

"Your mother moved in with you recently. Where did she live before?"

"On a commune in Mississippi. It's a farm, and she was a farmhand."

"Did you have a good relationship with her?"

"Yes. It was difficult for us to speak, since there weren't telephones, but when we did, we got along well."

"How did your mother know, Ms. McGreevy?"

"Ms. McGreevy ran the commune."

"You and Mr. Stevenson took a trip to Mississippi recently. What was its nature?"

"My mother called and said she was hurt, so we flew down there to help her."

"And you brought her back?"

"Yes, Sir. The night Momma and I were packing to leave, Ms. McGreevy kicked her door open and held us at rifle point. She didn't see Charlie standing behind her. So he grabbed her from behind and dragged her out. Ms. McGreevy fired a wild shot and it caught my mother's arm. There's a police report about all this. Anyway, under the circumstances, I'm sure you can see why we couldn't leave her there."

"Why did she stay there if they treated her that way?" Madigan asked while busy writing. Why didn't he just use a tape recorder?

I shouldn't have said anything unless my lawyer was present. Still, the faster I answer this man's questions, the quicker this can be over, and Momma can come home.

"Ms. McGreevy said that she should've killed Momma when she had the chance 'cause of what happened to Mr. Davenport."

Madigan's fingers traveled under his glasses to rub his eyes. "Who's Mr. Davenport?"

"The man who owned the farm. He disappeared and never came back. Then Ms. McGreevy owned it after that. Momma knew what happened and tried to tell the police, but Ms. McGreevy stopped her."

"How did she stop her?" His pen halted and he eyed me over his glasses.

"Blackmail, from what I could tell. Momma never talked about it with me, so I don't know what she held over her. But Ms. McGreevy said something about Momma agreeing to be a prisoner when we found her in my kitchen."

He wrote some more. "Okay, we'll have to check this out, and then someone will call you." He got up out of his seat.

I hoped to hell what I said helped, or else I got Momma into a whole heap of trouble.

# CHAPTER 35

Charlie's family gathered in the waiting room of the morgue when we got to the hospital. This included Sarah, who huddled with Bri and Connie. Charlie joined their group.

They lost their father because of my family's mess. None of them wanted to see me right now. Can't say I blamed them because I would've felt the same if I were in their shoes.

I went up to them and said, "I'm so very sorry for your loss. Please let me know if there's anything you need." They nodded half-heartedly while avoiding my eyes.

I moped to the corner of the waiting room, giving them their space to grieve.

Amberly, from the office, walked into the room and went over to Charlie, rested her head on his shoulder, and cried. As much as it killed me, I concealed my discomfort because this was all my fault, and Charlie probably blamed me.

She pulled away, looked up at him and said something. He bent and kissed the top of her head.

I rested my forehead against my hiked knees, wrapped my arms around my legs, and cocooned myself in my anguish as I cried miserably. For Ray. For Momma. For the Stevensons. And for me, who knew happiness for a little while before it was ripped away. Happiness never stayed.

Sometime later, I woke to an empty waiting room. The faint scent of Charlie's cologne hung in the air like a ghost, taunting me.

The events from last night, from Momma's broken plea to Charlie's wail at the sight of his dead father, settled in my brain.

The brutal ache in my heart made me want to crawl into bed for a few days. I hauled myself out of the chair. The fluorescent lights made me squint, and a sharp pain shot through my head from my stiff neck. I moved my stinging arm and groped for the phone in my pocket. The time on the screen read 5:47 a.m.

I used an app to order a taxi, then scrolled through

my messages to see if there were any from Charlie or even Sarah.

Nothing.

If I didn't feel shitty before, the absence of their messages left a slight panic in my gut. They needed time. They just lost their father.

*Because of me.*

* * *

It was 6:07 a.m. when the cabbie pulled up to my house. I paid with my phone, then got out of the cab and slammed the door. The rumble of the taxi pulling away behind me didn't distract my fixed gaze on the front door. My stomach tightened as I drew closer to the house and trudged up the driveway, steeling myself for what I was going to find.

I climbed the porch steps, expecting to see Ray's blood, but it was clean. The wood looked like it had been power washed. There was no stain at all—not even a chalk outline. The yellow police tape was taken off the door.

I inspected the houses on my block.

They did this?

An older neighbor to the left stepped out of his house in a blue robe over pajamas and waved at me. I waved back shyly, and he must have taken that as an invitation because he came over. I needed a hot shower and rest, but this was important. The neighbors required assurances that we weren't people who caused trouble.

"Hey there. Glad to see you got home okay. We were all worried about you," Mr. Nelson said. He usually wore glasses, but hadn't at the moment.

"Hi, Mr. Nelson. It's been a tough night."

"Everything okay with Gladys?" he cut to the chase.

Since Momma shared her Thanksgiving turkey recipe with Mr. Nelson's daughter, he'd been super friendly.

"She's in holding until everything checks out. They said it was a process that could take a few days."

He shook his head. "What happened? I heard shouting and was going to come over, but shots rang out, and I thought it best to hunker down. Who were the man and woman that were shot?"

*Thank God* he stayed in his house. It would've been awful if something happened to him. "The lady was the intruder who killed the man—Momma shot her."

"An intruder? That explains why my security lights kept going on all the time. Thought it was Reilly's cat."

He gestured with his chin to the house across the street.

My brain stopped for a second. Woah. What?

"How long has this been happening?" I asked.

"Every day, for about a month. I was about to head over there to see if something had happened to them since their cat was out so often."

"I'm so very sorry, Mr. Nelson." I shook my head while a rush of shame and helplessness filled my body. My wreck of a life affected so many people. It was like a family curse.

He smiled good-natured at me, making me feel worse. "I power washed your porch this morning and took down the police tape. You and Gladys didn't need to come home to that."

My eyes flooded with tears. No one had taken care of me like that.

Except for Charlie.

I placed my hand over my heart and said, "Thank you, Mr. Nelson. Mighty kind of you."

"No problem, darlin'. You go on and get some rest. Call me if you need anything."

I could only manage a shaky nod.

We said our goodbyes, I stepped inside and a chalk outline of Lynette's body greeted me. Her blood pooled on the tiled floor of the entryway, and some splattered on the walls. Anger surged through my veins, thinking about what that godforsaken bitch did to Charlie and my family.

I went straight into the kitchen's broom closet, side-stepping the groceries scattered across the floor. I grabbed the bucket and a scrub brush.

I squeezed dish detergent from the bottle into the water, and got to work. It was pushing me to the edge of my limits of exhaustion, but I couldn't rest knowing Lynette's outline and blood were there. It was like she was still in my house.

After removing the mess in the entryway, I picked up the groceries from off the floor.

Something caught my attention by the backdoor. I knelt by the door for a closer look. A block of wood had been nailed to the frame and positioned to stop the door from opening.

Wow. Just...fucking wow. This insane bitch. Why was it that after all that she'd done, her level of insanity never ceased to amaze me? It was one terrifying real-ization after another. Will it ever end?

I went to the toolbox in the broom closet, snatched my hammer, then pried the block from the back door.

# CHAPTER 36

**Carol Lynne Miller:** How are you? Where are you? I'm worried.

I sat on my bed, waiting for his response.

Nothing.

It was quarter past ten in the morning. He was probably busy at work. Lord knows that firm was probably in disarray.

*Poor Charlie.*

After washing up in the ensuite, I went downstairs to the living room and did some research for a side client. Even though the bed sang its siren song, promising hugs, warmth, and rest, I couldn't afford to stop working.

That nagging feeling clawed at my gut, and I'd changed tactics and phoned Charlie, before I lost my nerve.

No answer.

Shoving aside the dread, I went outside and brought in the newspaper that was tossed on the lawn.

Unfolding it as I came back inside the house, my stomach seized.

On the front page were pictures of Lynette and Ray. A shiver ran down my spine when seeing her. I placed my thumb over her face so that I didn't have to look at her, and concentrated on the article. The headline read:

*"Intruder Murdered Prominent Attorney During Home Invasion"*

I scanned the article. It gave a brief history of who Lynnette and Ray were, and some interviews from neighbors and passersby.

The thought of that block of wood flashed in my head again, and something bugged me about it. Maybe it was nothing, but I had a raging suspicion that needed checking out.

So I went upstairs to dress in warmer clothes, skipped my makeup routine, and put my long hair in a topknot. My blue jeans, creamy white turtleneck, black boots, and sporty black down jacket with a fur-trimmed hood were suitable for December in New York.

It occurred that I needed to do Christmas shopping, but I put it off since the key people in my life weren't here. That thought made my nose sting, so I banished it and got in my car.

I drove to the strip mall and parked in the lot with the Fresh Foods, along with a host of smaller stores.

The hardware store's door chimed when I pushed it open. It was small and crammed with items. Plastic packages hung along the wall, and some shelves were in the back, stacked with various items for household needs.

An older man with buzzed gray hair, wearing a navy blue sweater and an orange apron, peered over the top of his thick clear glasses. "Hello, can I help you find something?"

I answered, "Hello, Sir. I wondered if you'd seen this woman in this store." I placed the newspaper on the counter and pointed at Lynette's picture.

He examined the paper. "She's been in here." His expression sobered and morphed into concern and finally, alarm.

"She did that? Here?" He pointed to the headline.

With a sobered tone, I answered, "Yes, Sir. She broke into my house and shot that man to death." I pointed at Ray's photo. I wasn't sure how much to share, so I didn't elaborate further.

His eyes flew to mine.

I felt guilty for scaring him. "Long story. But she bullied my mother for years. Then she snapped and broke into my house."

His voice was rough. "She asked for nails, wood, and a hammer. Said she needed to fix her drawer. Told her she needed more than a woodblock and asked what kind of repairs the drawer needed. Then she got defensive and insisted she knew what she was doing."

I shook my head at that. "I'm sorry, Sir." Sorry he had to deal with her unpleasantness. He offered condolences for my loss. I thanked him, waved, and left.

I headed home after a trip to the florist to buy a bouquet for the kitchen table and a replacement carton of milk from Fresh Foods.

Mr. Nelson waved at me and walked up to my car as I pulled into my driveway. I stopped and lowered the passenger window. He bent his head and asked, "How's Gladys?"

"I don't know yet. I have to call the station to see."

"Okay, let me know how she's doing."

"Thanks for checking up on her. I'll let you know."

He nodded, straightened, and signaled that I should drive. Did he have a romantic interest in my mother, or was he always that friendly?

While inside my kitchen, I filled a crystal vase with water, unwrapped the flowers from the paper, and placed them in the vase.

Then I rested it on the table, took out my phone, and made a call.

When the voice on the other end greeted me, I said, "Hello, Detective Madigan. This is Carol Lynne Miller. You are holding my mother, Gladys Miller."

"Yes, Carol Lynne. How can I help you?" His tone sounded slightly put out.

"My back door was nailed shut with a block of wood when my mother and I tried to run out," I said.

"Yes, I'm aware of that."

"Well, when I'd removed it with my hammer, I noticed my toolbox was untouched. That had me wondering where Lynette got the nails from. So, I went to the hardware store and spoke to the clerk. He said that he remembered Ms. McGreevy."

"Okay. But I don't understand what that has to do with anything."

It was premeditated. Didn't he get that? Why would someone go through all that hassle if they weren't intending on killing? Therefore, Momma acted in self-defense.

Swear, he was so slow, it made me want to cross my eyes.

I needed a lawyer. More money. My spirits fell further.

"Sorry. Thought it would help Momma. Didn't mean to waste your time."

"No trouble at all, Ma'am. Call me if there's anything else I can do for you."

I thanked him and disconnected the call while expelling a swear. I required some sort of legal counsel.

Charlie's face flashed in my mind.

I opened my text screen.

**Carol Lynne Miller:** Thinking about you. Please call me, or text me, or come to see me as soon as you can. If it's better for me to go to you, let me know. Love you.

There was no response, and I didn't expect one. He was probably busy making funeral plans with his family. Speaking of which, I closed that message and opened the other person on my contact list.

**Carol Lynne Miller:** Hi, sweetheart. Just wanted to let you know that my thoughts are with you, Reese, and the babies. Please let me know if there's anything I can do to help.

I put the phone away and went to the living room to

search for a local lawyer on my laptop. After finding one with good reviews, I emailed them, then spent the rest of the day trying in vain to focus on work.

* * *

While reheating the leftover chicken casserole for supper that Momma had fixed a few nights ago. I stink-eyed the spot where Lynette stood drinking coffee while shoving my meal in my mouth, not really tasting it.

The way she'd done it so casually, as though she belonged here, both creeped me out and made my head want to explode.

Cleaning the floors to get rid of her wasn't going to cut it.

I needed fire.

After loading the dishwasher and turning it on, I wiped down the table and countertops.

Then I went into the living room and pulled open the drawer of the wooden sideboard. I grabbed my *Mantra Vajrasattva Chanting* CD, popped it in the ancient boombox, and turned up the volume.

The tranquil sound of the hang drum, beat a meditative rhythm while a woman's chanting filled the air. Immediately a sense of oneness filled my being. It was like every vibrational part of my body pulsed in time with the music.

I fished out the lighter from the drawer and lit several candles scattered around the living room.

The flame cast the room in warm light and shadows danced along the walls. It called to something soul-deep that twirled around my spirit and moved me with it.

I opened all the house windows to let the negative energies escape. A blast of December air that filtered through the house made me shiver.

Hanging on to the lighter, I searched through the drawer to find a brown soapstone smudge bowl and a bundle of white sage.

I lit the bundle and held it there for a second until the embers disappeared.

Its familiar aromatic herbal scent filled my lungs.

I ran the smoking sage along my body, purifying myself while my mind drifted into the meditative state of no thought beyond alertness.

Drifting into the kitchen, to the spot where Lynette stood, I waved the sage over the area. Then I moved to the entryway and porch and did the same.

Finally, I said a prayer of gratitude, and tossed it into the fireplace, leaving it to burn out.

After closing the windows, I blew out the candles.

Since it was now freezing, I lit a fire in the fireplace. The herbal aroma that permeated throughout the house made me feel centered.

After turning the volume of the chanting music down to a decent level, I wrapped myself in the throw from the couch.

I turned on my laptop and scrolled through my messages. An email from the lawyer said they were happy to take my case and suggested I call their office at my earliest convenience.

With half the load off my chest, I dialed the number.

# CHAPTER 37

I woke up the following day to the lingering scent of sage, which lightened the depression only a tad. After brushing my teeth, I dragged myself downstairs, spread my yoga mat by the bay window in the living room.

Then I did three sun salutations and, a quick chakra balance meditation that lasted a few minutes.

While having breakfast of toaster waffles, syrup, and a cup of coffee, I stared at the spot where Lynette stood. That heavy, grave vibe left the house.

After eating, I brought my breakfast dishes to the sink, then went upstairs and showered. Throwing on black yoga pants and a plain, slim black t-shirt with a sweetheart neckline, I was ready to take on the day.

Settling on the couch with the TV volume down low, I skimmed my daily agenda, and called the lawyer first.

While on hold for Kathy Markson, I responded to a few emails and made appropriate notes in my schedule.

"Hello, Ms. Miller? This is Kathy Markson."

"Hi, Kathy. Please, call me Carol Lynne."

"Carol Lynne, it is. I've read the preliminary information you've sent me over email, and I think you have a strong case. We are going to proceed by making a call to the Detective. I'll contact the police department in Mississippi and have them forward the police report that documented Ms. McGreevy breaking into your mother's residence brandishing a gun. This will show the break-in at your house was premeditated, and your mother had acted in self-defense."

"Thank you, Kathy. How long will all this take? As you can tell, I'm eager to get my mother home."

"Yes, I understand. It should take a few days to clear everything up."

My heart fell. She'll need to stay a few more days in jail.

"Okay. Thanks." It came out as dull as I felt.

We said our goodbyes and hung up.

Two days. Wow. There was no rushing this process. I just hope Momma didn't reckon that I abandoned her.

I scrolled through my texts. Zero from Charlie or Sarah and two from Ben.

We'd exceeded the maximum capacity at the venue. As a result, we'll need to cut back one of our vendors to not exceed the fire code.

I texted Ben, and we agreed to meet at the venue. Usually, this would've sent me into a spiral of stress. However, it just didn't seem that important, or at least, it didn't carry the same weight that it once had.

I headed up to my room and swapped my wide-legged pants for faded blue jeans that offered better protection against the frigid temperature.

* * *

Ben and the site manager, Jim Camen, waited for me in the lobby when I walked into Metro Hall. They were in the middle of discussing the capacity issue.

"I understand that there's a problem here, Sir." I broke into their conversation.

"You've exceeded the fire code with the number of people that will be in the building during the concert." Jim Camen explained. His tan suede jacket had brown patches. His side swept dark hair and glasses reminded me of Reese's stepdad. The reminder of not seeing or speaking with Sarah made a pang hit my heart.

I shoved all thoughts of her and her brother out of my head and focused on Jim and Ben. They sniffed the air, and I wrapped my arms around my torso. The scent of sage clung to my clothes. Something I no longer noticed, but others had. They probably thought I smoked weed.

"Your suggestion is to cancel a vendor?" I asked. Was he for real?

"Yes, it's the only way," Jim replied.

"No, it isn't! Especially when that vendor will make us money," I put in.

"What do you suppose we do? Cancel a ticket holder?" Ben smirked.

My eyes widened. I thought he was on my side.

We can't get rid of potential moneymakers. That would be crazy. "How about a crew member? We can ask one of them to stay home."

"You can't be serious!" Jim's eyes narrowed.

The first thing I threw out, but now, it made sense. "Very serious. I'd rather be short-staffed than cut off revenue. Plus, canceling our tickets may lead to bad press on social media. Cutting a vendor will take a chunk out of our sales. So the next step will be to lay off crew members and have someone else take over his job. We can pay them overtime or something for the setup or, better yet, have them start a day earlier."

Jim thought that over and sighed. "We need to re-sign the contract."

"We'll have to change the date, and we can both initial it." I offered.

He agreed, we pulled out our contracts, and initialed the change.

After we were done, I did something stupid.

Unbelievably stupid.

Let's just say it backfired…horribly.

# CHAPTER 38

The elevator doors opened on the eighth floor to SLS in gold letters, which stood for Stevenson Legal Services.

I crossed their pristine industrial blue carpet, to the cherry-wood receptionist's desk where Amberly Davidson usually sat, which was vacant.

She must have left, since it was Friday afternoon.

I made my way past the first set of double doors labeled Conference Room A.

The nameplate that read Charles Bradley Stevenson, directed me to the right place.

As I neared, a woman's laugh mixed with a man's came from within. "Sweetheart, it's been tough for you,

I know, but sometimes you need to make room for laughter. He would've wanted that."

Sweetheart? What the fuck?!

"I can always count on you to make me laugh. God knows I needed it."

That was Charlie!

What the FUCK?!

I flung the door open with such force that it vibrated when it crashed against the wall.

Amberly sat on his desk, legs crossed while Charlie reclined on his office chair. Both holding glass tumblers filled with some kind of liquor.

A fancy-ass decanter shimmered on his desk.

Almost empty.

They froze when their eyes caught mine. I probably looked like a dragon, about to eviscerate them with my hellfire.

"Now I know why you don't have time to talk to me! You don't want anything to do with me. I get it! But you could've been man enough to FUCKING say something instead of ghosting me!"

My hand itched with an overwhelming need to throw that fucking decanter through the window.

So. Fucking. Much.

But I couldn't afford to pay for the damages.

I about-faced and ran the hell out of there.

A bright red tag labeled the fire exit over the side door flashed like a beacon. No way I wanted to stand there waiting for the elevator.

I made it down the stairs, and through a metal door that led out to the street. Luckily, my car was parked a little way up the road.

I swiped at my tears, hating them. Didn't need fucking tears right now.

I got to my car, ripped open the door, got in, started it, and maneuvered out of the parking spot. The tires squealed when I mashed the gas pedal.

It took over an hour to drive to Monroe. Sitting in traffic on the George Washington Bridge didn't help calm me down one bit. It made it worse because I cried and hated myself for every wasted tear.

And it made it worse because my phone blew up, so I turned it off and tossed it on the passenger seat.

At least I didn't have to wonder anymore. He doesn't want to talk to me or see me again. I can accept that and move on as much as it'll kill me. And I won't run into him—maybe if I'm visiting Sarah.

If she'll ever speak to me.

My stomach turned.

Fucking Lynette. I hope she's burning in hell.

I wanted to crawl out of my skin. To be someone else. Somewhere else. Something else.

Needing to divorce from my mind for a little while, I drove around town until I found a bar called "The Lucky Trio."

I scored a parking spot on the street in front of the place, got out, and fed the meter for two hours. That should get me nice and sloshed.

Inside the bar, boat paddles hung crisscrossed on the far wall, along with a scattering of framed pictures. Booths occupied the right side of the room, and a bar occupied the left.

Charming.

I waved at the middle-aged bartender and pointed to the booths. He nodded, which I took to mean that I could choose any unoccupied one to sit down.

Supper was a good idea since I intended to drink a lot. Other than the occasional glass of wine, I wasn't much of a drinker. Maybe I could try a cocktail.

While shrugging off my coat and tossing it in the booth, an older blonde server whose name tag read "Luanne" placed a menu in front of me.

"Hey there. What can I getcha?"

The table card had a picture of a coffee martini, which sounded yummy, so I selected that.

"How about a coffee martini?"

She nodded and asked, "Anything else?"

I glanced through the pictures on the menu and

ordered a Swiss and mushroom burger and mozzarella sticks.

I hadn't eaten since breakfast, so it was understandable that I gobbled it down and slung back the martini like it was water. Charlie would've cracked up if he saw me eating meat.

*Cringe.* Charlie.

Feeling drained, I paid for my meal, put on my coat, and headed back to my car. Driving wasn't too tricky since The Lucky Trio was only a few minutes away from my house.

When I pulled into the driveway, a familiar car was parked in front of the house, and a person was sitting on the porch steps.

My heart plummeted.

I parked in the garage, then headed to the front of the house. As I approached the porch, the pleasantly numb state that the drink brought on had vanished. I prepared myself to fight.

When I rounded the corner, the person stood up. I recognized that silhouette and could pick it out of a crowd of a thousand.

Tears filled my eyes, and I gulped in cool air to relax my tight throat.

"Go home, Charlie."

"Funny thing. Home. Where the hell do you go

when you're not sure where yours is?" he asked in a broken voice.

I walked past him to the door, taking my keys out of my pocket.

Charlie said nothing as I tried to find the right keys to insert in the locks. Not being familiar with them, the dark, and my shaking hands aided my struggle. I wanted to get this over with, so he can leave, and I can—

*God.*

Spiral into the abyss of depression.

I pushed open the door, and he followed me inside, flipping on the lights. Then Charlie marched straight into the kitchen and flipped on the lights there. He looked around and went to the back door and pulled it open like he was testing it.

Charlie walked off to the side, and it sounded like he opened the basement door.

I shrugged off my coat and hung it in the closet. Then I slipped out of my boots and placed them on the mat. Not understanding what was going on and feeling fed up with this whole situation, I flopped on my couch. Placing my phone on the coffee table, I opened my laptop and checked my mail. There was a message from the lawyer that said I should call her.

I scrolled to the lawyer's contact and hit the call

button. Charlie walked into the living room, took off his coat, opened the coat closet, and hung it up.

Why, though? He wasn't staying.

On the phone, a voice mail recording urged me to leave a message. "Hello, this is Carol Lynne Miller. I'm sorry we had missed each other. I was dealing with a work emergency and saw your message. Please call me anytime." I shut my eyes. That'll teach me to turn my phone off.

Charlie ran up the stairs. My knees bounced as the ceiling creaked with the sound of his footsteps.

I shouldn't have to feel this way! Dang it! Why couldn't he say what he had to and leave?!

I shot up and marched up the stairs.

Found him in my bedroom, testing the windows.

"What the hell are you doing?!"

"What does it look like?" He ignored me and continued opening and closing the window.

What fucking answer was that?

"Why are you here?" My voice didn't betray my inner shakiness.

"Cause you won't fucking listen."

What?!

"Listen to what? I'd been texting you for FUCKING days! Come to find out that you had already moved on and didn't have the balls to tell me."

He stopped, and glared murderously.

If he thought it could intimidate me, he had another thing coming. I fucking had it with him, and he can get the fuck out of my house.

"I get it, Charlie! You never want to see me again because your father died, and it's my fault."

What little control I'd possessed flew out the window, and my tears spilled over.

His eyes bulged like he couldn't believe what came out of my mouth. "That's what you'd been thinking?" he asked, sounding exasperated.

I took a breath and said, "Believe me, if I could have traded places with him, I would—in a second."

He advanced on me with a fierce look in his eyes. With both hands on my cheeks, he said, "Don't you ever fucking say that. Ever."

That broke through my haze. Shock replaced misery as I replayed what he said, trying my damnedest to understand.

"He died because of me." I repeated in case he didn't understand me the first time.

He lowered his voice to a painful whisper. "He died because of me, not you."

What? How did that make any sense?

Charlie went on to explain. "We got into an argument at work, and he followed me here to patch things up. If I had self-control, shit wouldn't have gotten out of hand, and he wouldn't have been here. It was also my fault Lynette broke in. I should have seen this house had better locks. I should've protected you better." His eyes welled up, and tears ran down. He focused on my chin.

"Charlie." I choked out.

None of that was his fault. Didn't he understand that?

I wrapped my arms around his waist. "This tragedy had nothing to do with you. Lynette had broken in because she was obsessed with controlling my mother. For years. This was my fault. My family's problem."

I soothed his back, and he wrapped himself around me like he wanted to crawl inside my body.

And I let him.

My strong, charming, solid man broke down.

He positioned his nose by my neck while his body shook with a silent sob.

It gutted me, and I cried, while guilt ate me up.

I missed him.

So much.

Charlie's fingers searched my head to feel the top bun. He pulled on the elastic so that my hair spilled down. Tossing the band aside, he ran his fingers through my hair, inhaled, and moaned.

Charlie's body molded to mine, and he kissed a trail to my lips. Then his hungry mouth took mine. His tongue rediscovered and reclaimed. My lips burned because of it.

Pulling apart, we undressed with urgency.

After we were naked, he lifted me, and I wrapped my legs around his waist. He carried me to the bed and tossed me down. Then he fell on top of me seconds later and continued kissing with a fever I'd never felt.

Charlie wrapped my legs high around his waist, positioned himself, and sunk his cock deep into me. We filled the room with mixed sounds of our moans. He buried his face in my neck, inhaled, and moved his hips.

Being so full all at once, it took a moment to get reacquainted.

He picked up the pace, fucking me hard with his entire body like he was possessed. I raised my legs higher and tipped up my hips to feel him deeper.

He grunted in my ear. Savage. Hot. Everything.

A beast was attacking me in the most beautiful way. My whole body was on fire as he moved, and the first shiver rippled through my walls.

Charlie cried in response and moved faster, encouraging my release.

I pressed my head into the bed, not able to hold on

any longer. My body exploded in a fiery sensation, quaking as beads of sweat rolled from my forehead.

Charlie lost control, his strokes were shallow. With a roar his body seized and warmed my walls.

He laid on top of me for a while, his heavy breath blew in my ear.

I caressed his broad back, loving the feel of this hulk of a man on top of me.

Safety. Warmth. Oneness.

Charlie moved to the side and wrapped his arm around my waist. Then he brought the covers over us and held me close while we fell asleep.

He woke me in the middle of the night for more lovemaking. This time, it was slow and so filled with so much beauty, our tears leaked.

That weekend, he mentioned he was headed to the hardware store to change the locks on my exterior door.

I told him that he should have a set of keys made for himself while there, and bring his clothes from his apartment. That earned me a huge, gorgeous smile and kisses, which turned into another lovemaking session.

We must have made love a dozen times over that weekend, so I couldn't pinpoint the exact day we conceived our daughter, Olivia.

# CHAPTER 39

The funeral was put off for a week until Saturday because of a delay in getting the medical examiner's report, which frustrated the hell out of Charlie.

Bri and Sarah were handling the reception at Ray's apartment. Even though he was well-known, they were planning an intimate funeral.

The silver lining was that Momma's legal problems got sorted, according to the phone call I received from the lawyer.

I texted a message to Bri and asked if they needed help.

No response.

Next, I sent a text to Sarah.

**Carol Lynne Miller:** Hon, please let me know if I can do anything to help you and Bri prepare for the funeral service.

**Sarah Malone:** No thanks, we're good.

I tried not to read into it, but how could I not? Charlie was stressed at work and with making funeral arrangements, so I couldn't go to him. Adding my emotional drama with his sisters wasn't right.

On Wednesday, I received a call from Detective Madigan saying I could pick up Momma. I drove over to the station as soon as we ended the call, not wanting her to stay there.

When I arrived at the police station, the front desk stayed empty for a half-hour until an officer showed up. Impatience didn't look good on me, so I had to force calmness to not delay the release process further.

I couldn't sign the release papers fast enough, and had to wait another maddening ten minutes for an officer to usher my mother out from the back.

Momma hobbled, her face was drawn, and dark circles colored around her eyes.

My heart ached. For everything she'd faced all her life, she didn't need this. If I wasn't so selfish and escaped to college, she wouldn't have had to stay there. I could've gone to school locally, so she could move in.

That little voice in my head told me that Lynette wouldn't have made it that easy. In my heart of hearts, I knew she would have put up a fight, and no way I could've won it without Charlie's help.

While I wrapped my arms around my mother, my chin wobbled. I hoped that in my embrace, she knew that I had her back and wouldn't ever let her down again. Her body bobbed in my arms as she sobbed.

"I'm sorry, Momma. So very sorry." My voice cracked. "But everything's done and over. You can be at peace knowing that no one will hurt you again."

She sobbed harder, her body heaving with it.

It was like all the stress she'd carried for years, seeped out. And it broke my heart.

When she regained control, we left the station.

I had to deal with the capacity problem, so as much as I hated it, I drove into the city to deal with it, leaving Momma in the car.

A few days later, I took her to *Glow* because it was healthy for her to get out and talk to people. I introduced her to Cheryl, and they hit it off. Momma told her she lived on a commune, and Cheryl shared she lived on one briefly during the mid-seventies in California–a surprise to me because she never mentioned it in the few years I shopped here.

To my delight, they exchanged numbers before we left, and I ended up buying some more Sage.

I wanted to do something special for her but knew she wasn't up to going out, so I ordered Chinese takeout and invited Mr. Nelson to join us for supper.

While we ate at the kitchen table, Charlie was warm enough but quiet. And I got it. I really did. But it made me pick at my food.

"How were you able to cook everything on time?" Mr. Nelson asked my mother.

"We made everything in large base batches and altered the recipes for variation."

"Wow," he laughed like she blew his mind.

I wasn't sure they should talk about the farm in front of Charlie, since it must've reminded him of Lynette. But he said nothing about it. His silence made me realize what we were up against. We'll always have this horrible thing between us.

Trying not to add an extra thing to worry about, I shoved that thought out of my head.

Desperate to jog Charlie out of his head, I asked, "How's everything going at work?" I placed my hand on Charlie's arm while Mr. Nelson and Momma were in a world of their own.

"I reassigned my work to the juniors. Troy, Richard, and I have taken on," he gulped, "Dad's cases. What about you? Have you gotten the capacity issue cleared yet?"

I frowned when he mentioned his father, but forged on and answered his question. "Yes, I drove in this morning and fixed everything. We don't have to lose vendors, but we'll lose crew members. It pissed off the owner because it meant that some of his people would not be paid, and being so close to Christmas was totally jacked up. Those were the breaks, I guess."

Although tempted, I didn't ask if his sisters needed help. It felt like a no-go subject with him. He didn't sleepover that night or any nights leading up to the funeral. That should've been my first clue that shit was about to go down.

# CHAPTER 40

I drove to the cemetery in Queens with Momma and Mr. Nelson. He sat in the back seat and talked about his late wife, Pattie, who passed away from breast cancer eight years ago.

I tried to pay attention to their conversation, but I couldn't. Instead, my mind wandered to last night when I texted Charlie to ask if he still wanted us there.

His reply text was, "Sure thing, Shug." That was it. I spent the rest of our car ride dissecting why he'd been standoffish.

Usually warmer when we spoke, his aloofness worried me. But I had to tell myself that he was busy tending to Ray's final arrangements and dealing with the law firm, he couldn't communicate the way he used to.

I clung to that belief with all my might because I drove myself nuts with this shitty feeling of uncertainty that had lived in my gut lately.

After the GPS guided us to a parking spot, we stopped at a street vendor to buy a bouquet of lilies to place by the grave.

Cars streamed past the open gates of the cemetery. The chilly December wind caused my hair to billow. I wrapped my arms around my body as I led the way. Momma and Mr. Nelson followed close behind.

A large group of people towards the right side, inward toward the cemetery's northend, milled about.

As we'd drawn closer, I picked out a few familiar faces in the crowd. Connie, Ray's girlfriend, stood with a tall, brown-haired woman. Bri. Her long, black coat molded to her baby bump.

Sarah and Reese were easy to spot because they held their twins. Her brush-off hurt. Not only had I done so much for her as far as pushing her towards her career, but if it weren't for me, she would have never met Reese.

After all, I set them up on their first date and deserved more credit than how she treated me. She was grieving the loss of her father, and that was why I didn't confront her. But dang, she was family. They all were–

Was that Amberly with her arms around Charlie?

Fuck!

*Not now.*

Momma must have seen them too because I heard her intake of breath.

Mr. Nelson stopped speaking for a second, then he let out a disappointed sigh.

"Let's stay, pay our respects, and go home. I have work that I need to tend to in the City," I said in a brittle tone.

Charlie eased her away as he walked over to his sisters and wrapped his arms around the two of them. Amberly followed close behind, then said something to Sarah while rubbing her arm. Sarah smiled and inclined her head.

Amberly glanced in our direction and said something to her group. Judging by the set of her jaw, I could tell it wasn't pleasant. Sarah eyed us.

Charlie swung his head around in our direction. His dark, designer sunglasses hid his eyes, so I couldn't read his expression. He left his family and walked over to us with determined strides.

No, no, no.

My gloved hands gripped the bouquet harder.

He drew closer.

I steeled myself against whatever he was about to say.

He reached out, drew me into his arms, and crushed me against him. "I need you by my side all the time. Never leave me again," he whispered in my ear.

Hiding my shock behind my scrunched face, I hoarsed out, "I never left. You never visited or indicated you wanted to see me. Besides, you were making out well without me." I pointed my chin at Amberly.

Charlie pulled back and gawked at me. "I'm a lawyer, so I have to act tough as though nothing phases me, no matter what."

I guess we were going to have this conversation here, of all places. "That was not what I meant. You were very cozy with that woman. You don't need me here." My eyes and throat stung despite my bravery.

He rested his black, leather-gloved hands on my shoulder. "She has been annoying the shit out of me lately. I wanted her to leave, but she has been hanging around since Dad passed. Don't know how to tell her to go away. Trying very hard not to be an asshole, but my patience is wearing thin."

My jaw dropped.

While I stood speechless, he gave Momma a hug.

Then he shook Mr. Nelson's hand. "Nice to see you, Grant. Thanks for coming."

"Thanks for inviting us," Mr. Nelson replied.

He invited Mr. Nelson? When? I had to send him a text message to check if I was invited, but Mr. Nelson got an invitation?

Okay. I needed to stop. I took a steadying breath to calm my foolish thoughts.

Charlie wrapped his arm around my shoulder and led us over to the crowd. I slung mine around his waist as we walked together, grateful for the support.

As we approached, Amberly's face fell, while Bri and Sarah frowned. My arm fell from his waist as I tried to pull away, but his vise-like grip kept me in place.

I focused on the mahogany casket and breathed in the chilly December air. Its coolness burned my nose, and for the oddest reason, I loved it.

A man wearing a long, black coat and holding a bible spoke up, and a hush fell over the crowd. "We are here today to pay our tribute and our respect to a beloved father, a brother, and mentor, Raymond Cedric Stevenson. To know Raymond was to love him, for it was from his loving guidance that we found grace and peace.

"Raymond Cedric Stevenson, we wish you well and thank you for being a part of our lives. We honor your life on Earth, and we pray for your peace ever after. We will not forget you. Go well."

He said a prayer and ended it with Amen.

While the mechanism lowered the casket into the grave, Charlie's body trembled. I placed my other hand on his chest to steady him. There were a few sniffles that came from the side, which I assumed were Ray's daughters.

After the casket rested in the ground, everyone took turns tossing their bouquets on top.

I left Charlie's side to toss in my lilies. When done, he pulled me back in his embrace and clung to me.

The mourners hugged Charlie, Sarah, and Bri then filed out. Momma and Mr. Nelson came up to us.

"I can drive your car back home while you stay with Charlie," Mr. Nelson offered.

Charlie asked with his brows drawn, "You drove here? I didn't even think about how you got here. Sorry, love."

His declaration seeped through my body, warmed my heart, and caused me to smile.

I said, "It's okay. You had a lot on your mind. I understand."

He whispered to me. "None of which is more important than you."

My heart melted. Then he kissed the top of my head.

Momma smiled.

Mr. Nelson prompted, "Carol Lynne. Keys?"

I reached into my coat pocket, pulled my keys, and tossed it to him.

Charlie said, "She'll stay with me. We'll be back sometime on Sunday."

My body heated, and I'm pretty sure my face pinked. Praise Jesus for the cold, which I'll blame on it.

"I'll have supper ready for y'all," Momma offered.

I spoke up. "Actually, I can't make it on Sunday because of the concert. I'll be working. You'll see me on Monday. Call if you need anything."

# CHAPTER 41

## CHARLIE

Entering Dad's apartment for the reception did weird shit to me. His presence filled the room with warmth and comfort, and it felt like he hadn't left. I kept expecting him to walk out of his office to tell us he ordered food from downstairs, and it should be up in a half-hour.

Going into his office to find his birth certificate and social security card was awful, but unavoidable, because my sisters couldn't have handled it. Essie fell to pieces, and Bri took care of her, which had helped. The only person who hung around me was Amberly.

*She wasn't the one I needed.*

The hippy, my sugar, my Carol Lynne became essential to my peace of mind.

The night-and-day difference between them startled me. Amberly came off as desperate and clingy.

The comfort and warmth that Carol Lynne radiated were like nothing I'd ever experienced. She infused me with peace. Even when all the crazy shit went down around her, her energy made me feel grounded for the first time in my life.

Crazy as that sounded.

My cousin, Renee, walked up to us and hugged both Carol Lynne and me. "I didn't get a chance to talk to you at the burial. Sorry about everything." She asked Carol Lynne, "How did you know Uncle Ray?"

"Renee, this is my girlfriend, Carol Lynne."

Renee's brows drew together like she was figuring out a puzzle. Then she straightened her expression, nodded, and greeted Shug. After she left, we went to my sisters and brothers-in-law, where they were talking to Amberly.

"Hey, guys," I broke into their conversation.

"Amberly told us about her exploits being a Lumberjack in Oregon," Essie piped up.

"For real. That's badass, yo," Reese said while looking around the room, probably to locate which of our relatives held his pint-sized menaces.

Troy remained stone-faced because he knew about it, seeing as Amberly was his ex. I bet Bri didn't know about their past because she wouldn't be so chummy with her.

Carol Lynne's face filled with longing, like she wanted to talk to my sister, while Es ignored her.

And it fucking killed me.

My sister never healed from losing her fiancé and baby until she met Carol Lynne and later, Reese. My woman helped to push Es' life on track, and of all people, she deserved better than this.

I bit out, "Es, can I talk to you outside, please?" Gesturing with my hand for her to follow, I led her around the throng and out of the apartment, and I closed the door behind us.

"What's up with you and Carol Lynne?"

Her brows knitted. "What do you mean?"

"Why are you keeping her at a distance?"

Her face fell, finally understanding my point. "Charlie. I can't right now, okay? She needs to be patient."

I exploded. "She *is* patient! You're being a bitch!"

Her gray eyes widened, then watered.

"You don't handle pain well. Everyone in this family knows that. But shit! You owe Carol Lynne, of all people, pretty much everything you have. She stood by you when you shut yourself out of family life. This is how you repay her?"

"I'm—I—"

I interrupted her sputter.

"What happened to Dad wasn't her fault. It wasn't Gladys's fault either. It was that psycho's fault. Don't fucking lay the blame on victims. Or did you forget you said the same thing to Bri and me when you turned your back on us? Not to mention on Dad too."

"How is it that you can demand people treat you one way, but you're not willing to do the same for others? What do you think Dad would say if he saw you being like this to her?"

She put her hands up to cover her face and cried because we both knew what he would have said.

Reese opened the door and went to Es. "What the hell, bro? We heard you shouting inside," he said to me.

"Talking sense into my sister. You can take it from here."

I stormed back into the apartment when Amberly hurried up to me.

"Charlie, I'm so sorry that you're upset."

"Yeah," I replied while scanning the room for Carol Lynne.

"Sweetie, maybe you need to leave and get some rest."

"Not until I find my *girlfriend* first. She's the only person I want to see," I said through my teeth.

She stopped, and her face fell. I'd never been blunt to her, but she hadn't taken my previous hints, and I was damned tired. Today of all days, I didn't have the strength. She nodded and walked away. I exhaled and closed my eyes for a second as relief ran through my body.

Shug's blond hair made her easy to spot in a crowded room. Her head, bent, while in conversation with my cousin, Lauren. Bri was by herself, over by the window, staring out while Troy approached Amberly. Sarah and Reese walked into the room, fetched their kids from Marcy and Joan, and went to Bri. They said something and hugged, then left the reception. My heart gave a guilty pang for how I yelled at Sarah.

Shit!

I rubbed the back of my neck. I wasn't handling this well.

After the reception, I drove Carol Lynne to the venue, where she got shit sorted for the concert the next day. I sat in my car and waited for her, even though it took a few hours. I needed time to get my head straight and think of a way to make things up to Es.

# CHAPTER 42

CAROL LYNNE

"All's well, boss." I smiled as Ben's voice came through my headset. This concert ran smoother than that last one.

On the last of my rounds, I knocked on the dressing room door of Sonic Wave before walking in. The musicians huddled together on the couch, speaking into a skinny, silver mic a reporter pointed towards them.

I waved and gave my thumbs up to everyone. They waved back, and I backed out of the room, closing the door behind me.

Allowing the press backstage before the start of the concert got us extra publicity. I hoped it would solidify Firelight Production's brand visibility to the venue owners and the biggest obstacle, the talent.

As I walked down the hall and onto the stage, I looked out at the crammed crowd. They wore band t-shirts and excited faces.

Folding my fingers into a rock symbol, I lifted it.

An eruption of cheers broke out.

That electrifying rush zinging through my body—

Fucking Awesome.

Off to the side, my eyes caught on Charlie with his arm around a brunette talking to a taller man.

My heart plummeted to my feet. Hurt and fury dueled for first place as I marched across the stage and down towards the gated partition, then stopped and took a deep breath.

*My Charlie wouldn't let me down.*

I focused on the tall man, then the brunette. My face grew cold.

*Shit.*

The events of the reception filled my head as I made my way to them.

"Hey, you guys."

All eyes were on me, and their jovial expressions morphed to contrition.

Sarah left her brother's side, rushed up with her arms spread wide, and then folded me in an enormous hug.

"I'm so sorry, sweetheart," she said in my ear.

I shut my eyes. "Thank you." I tightened my arms and rubbed her back. Then I pulled away as something occurred. "Where are the kids?"

"We dropped them off at Reese's mom's."

Unfortunately, I couldn't stay with them for too long because I needed to check on the vendors.

After the concert, they headed home.

Charlie took me back to his apartment. Too tired to move, we'd collapsed into each other's arms and fell asleep.

By the time I walked into Charlie's living room Monday morning, he had already left for work.

There were two dozen roses in a crystal vase sitting on his dining room table. A small card with an embossed filigree design read:


*Congratulations on a job well done, Shug.*


  *Love,*
  *Charlie*

# CHAPTER 43

We were still in our pajamas when I led Charlie outside to the driveway on Christmas morning. His face lit up when we approached the freestanding basketball hoop.

"I don't want you to lose out on your friendships because you're living here."

Charlie's eyes glowed with tenderness.

It touched my heart, infiltrated my lungs, and seeped into my bones where it warmed me.

"Baby, this is the sweetest thing anyone has ever given me." He lifted me and we kissed deeply.

After he put me down, Charlie pulled an envelope out of his back pocket, winked, and said, "Merry Christmas."

My brows scrunched together. I opened it, and yanked out the paper that looked like a mortgage statement.

I scanned it, not understanding what it was.

It took a second before realizing I held *my* mortgage statement.

The bottom showed a zero balance.

Then it hit.

My eyes rounded, my mouth dropped open, and a gasp fell out.

Charlie wore an ear-to-ear grin.

I jumped into Charlie's arms, burying my face in his neck, and sobbed.

He held me, his body moved with laughter, its richness sounded in my ear.

And that paled to the biggest shock, which came later that day.

Christmas day was subdued. Sarah and Reese dropped by for a few hours and had lunch with us.

Momma made oven-roasted turkey with cider gravy, pull-apart rolls, and creamed butterbean.

I'd been feeling off for the following few days when I finally did something about it.

That evening, I stood by the doorway of the ensuite, taking a second to admire my man.

Charlie leaned against the headboard, working on

his laptop. The screen illuminated his square jaw and the perfection of his face.

He looked up, and we locked eyes. His eyes drifted to the pregnancy test I held, and it took a second for them to bulge.

Charlie moved his laptop to the side table, got out of bed, and gathered me in a hug. He lifted me, and I wrapped my legs around his waist.

Our lips pressed, his tongue teased mine as he walked us to our bed where he laid me down.

Charlie took the pregnancy stick and examined the positive display. With a smile, he rested it on the table, and then tore off his white t-shirt and blue plaid pajama pants, revealing his muscled, naked body.

When I moved to do the same, he brushed my hand away and said, "Let me."

Charlie removed my red, spaghetti-strapped pajama top and matching shorts with such gentleness, my eyes welled.

I rested my palm on his cheek. He took my hand, brought it to his lips, and pressed a kiss on my finger-tips. Then he placed my palm against his heart as tenderness filled his eyes, communicating unspoken words.

*Beautiful.*

The fire burned that behind Charlie's intense gaze ignited a similar one in my core.

He dragged my hand down his sculpted chest to his six-pack abs and down further to his thick shaft.

I wrapped my hand around him and squeezed, then moved it back and forth. I kissed the smooth tip and looked at him suggestively.

Charlie's lips broadened with a naughty smile, which I took as encouragement, so I licked the tip.

He expelled a breath.

Before I knew it, he grabbed me by the wrist, made me unhand him, and shoved me backward, so I laid flat on my back.

Charlie raised my feet so they rested on his broad shoulders. Then he locked his arm around my leg, positioned himself at my entrance, and thrust in.

Our harmonic groans filled the air.

Charlie's fierce eyes held mine as he rocked his hips maddeningly slow, building a fire.

He graveled out, "You are my love, my world, and my heart's desire."

Before I could even react, he lifted my legs and moved faster, making me forget my words.

My chin tilted up as a moan escaped my lips.

Charlie leaned forward and palmed my breast

causing my nipples to tingle and harden as they rubbed against his skin.

He picked up his pace, his body clapped into mine as though we were applauding.

Charlie grunted, "Tell me you love me."

"I love you," I pleaded in a garbled voice. The intensity in my core was too much to take.

He leaned forward and hammered hard, and my toes curled in response. Then, with a gasp, I let go. My body vibrated as heat washed in waves.

Charlie gritted his teeth as he shuttered, releasing his warmth, then collapsed beside me.

We sounded like a pair of runners.

A smile spread across his face, and he rested a hand on my damp stomach. "Best Christmas present. *Ever.*"

# EPILOGUE

I huddled with Momma and Mr. Nelson—who I now called Grant since he became my stepfather nine years ago. We smiled as I snapped a selfie while the other parents filed into the gym for the school's Christmas recital.

When Charlie walked through the gym doors, I waved.

He saw us, smiled, and shuffled through the row of seats to get to us.

Like always, women gave my husband appreciative glances as he walked by. It was something that I got used to after ten years of being married to this gorgeous man. The few gray hairs that grew along the side of his head made him more distinguished.

*Sigh.*

Some people had all the luck.

Our three-year-old son, Gabriel, sprawled on my lap while looking at the Christmas decorations with disinterest.

When I waved at his father, he looked over and straightened.

Charlie nodded at Grant and leaned down to kiss Momma's cheek before picking up our son, who made grabby hands at him.

I removed our coats from the reserved seat.

Once he got settled, Charlie leaned over, and pecked me on the lips.

I snapped a selfie of us posing with our youngest. Then Charlie took the phone and snapped another of him kissing the top of my head.

We took lots of pictures because when our kids grow up, they'll have something to look back on.

Their childhood events were commemorated.

Their histories, documented.

I gave them something I never had.

Charlie wanted to fill an album with us kissing, so our kids could see how much their dad loved their mom.

My sweet man. Can't get enough of him. Never could.

After Momma moved next door with Grant, we renovated our basement so that our daughter, Olivia, had a safe place to play. It was completed soon after I gave birth to our middle child, Ray.

We'd decided our family was complete after the birth of Gabe four years later.

Since then, ballet classes, little league, and music classes filled our lives.

Charlie sold his father's practice and opened up a new one five minutes from our house so he didn't have a far commute to work.

I didn't keep up with my concert producer gig because family life became too hectic.

And I didn't miss it *at all*.

These days I looked forward to family events, like the Christmas craft fair happening tomorrow. Olivia donated a few pecan pies that she baked with the help of her Meemaw.

As for the rest of the Stevensons, Sarah and I were never as close as we once were. However, she and her brother had gotten closer. She brought her twins over when she had time off from her seaside bistro, but life pulled us apart.

Bri visited occasionally because she was busy raising her son and 'fighting the good fight,' as she called it, which meant being a judge. She was no longer married to Troy, and praise Jesus for that.

What an insane story.

Poor Amberly.

None of us saw it coming. It had messed up Charlie for a while because he felt guilty for his part. Soon after Ray's funeral, we found out what a monster Troy had been to Amberly and Bri.

We last saw Amberly back at the trial. Judging by that super-hot guy with her, I'd say things turned out fine for her.

The gym lights dimmed, and a hush fell over the audience. The spotlight shone on Liv as she emceed her school's Christmas concert. Everyone laughed, to my relief, at the jokes she'd worked so hard on at home.

The curtains had risen, and Ray's class filled the stage. They put on their sunglasses and sang *Jingle Bell Rock*.

* * *

*Timber Wolf (Elements of Danger Book 3)*

*Timberwolf*

**It takes triggering one closely guarded secret to end everything.**

**She needs to rebuild her life...**
Amberly Davidson survives a horrific assault by a man she once loved. Her mother brings her back home to Oregon. Her mother never mentioned that the family business, a sawmill, is in hot water because a rival company is looking to shut them down.

**He can't repeat his former mistakes...**

Jackson Kent, a sinfully gorgeous tree feller, fights his attraction to Amberly because her mother led him to believe that Amberly has a drinking problem and got into a car accident to explain her bruises from the assault.

Amberly must fight to pull the business out of choppy waters, and fight her attraction to her co-worker, Jackson Kent. Can Jax lead Amberly to trust him, or will his secret destroy them? And then there's her attacker, who calls her from jail. Will she ever be free of him?

*The content in this book may be triggering for some readers as it contains murder, stalking and violence. It is intended for readers 18+.*

* * *

*If you enjoyed this book, please consider leaving a review.*

* * *

*Sign up for my newsletter and receive "Sea Legs
Point Five," Free!*

After a party where she gets drunk, her best friend
convinces her to go on three blind dates. She meets
Reese Malone on her third date. He's *the guy*.

**But First. There was this guy...**

Meet Melvin—the first of Sarah's three dates.

# TIMBERWOLF
### (EXCERPT FROM TIMBERWOLF, CHAPTER 1

## Chapter 1
## Amberly Davidson

Someone knocked on my bedroom door while I slumped at my desk, scrolling through Chirp Vox headlines on my laptop. In my red pajamas with tiny Christmas trees printed on them, I got up and answered the door.

"Merry Christmas, Chica." Marisol Rodriguez, my roommate, stood by the doorway wearing a white tank and gray sweatpants. Her arm was extended holding a red envelope. Her vivid hazel eyes were set off by caramel skin and matching tight, wild, corkscrew curls. Marisol's doll-like appearance was a few inches shorter than my 5'6. Her petite frame made me feel like the Hulk in comparison. I was what some would consider voluptuous, but I felt dumpy most of the time.

I arranged my lips in a smile and hoped it didn't look like a grimace, then said, "Merry Christmas to you too." I took her Yuletide offering, went over to my desk and rifled through a stack of unopened Christmas cards to locate hers in the letter basket where my mail was stashed.

"You planning on doing anything for today?" Marisol asked. Her eyes roamed to my tinsel-less walls in my jam-packed bedroom—a contrast to her festive one. She knew I wasn't filled with cheer, because she walked in on me crying over Mr. Stevenson's death last week and helped me when Charlie showed up at our door. Since then, I didn't have the strength for much. The fact that I wore my Christmas pajamas demon-strated effort.

I grabbed her envelope and handed it to her. "Prob-ably going to phone my mom and watch TV all day," I answered.

She tilted her head and said, "*¡Oye!* You can come with me to my friend Carlotta's. She cooks *un* *desayuno auténtico de Puerto Rico.*" Authentic Puerto Rican breakfast.

"Sounds delicious, but I don't feel like going out right now. Thanks for the offer, though."

She pinched her lips and her gaze traveled down to my pajamas. "But I leave in an hour, if you change your mind, okay?" Her accent was heavy, but her English was coming along. She'd been living here for five years and had taught me a good deal of Spanish as well.

"Okay, *gracias.*"

The honest grin that spread across her lovely face lifted my mood a smidge. She did that when I attempted to speak Spanish. If it made her happy, then why not?

After she left, I closed the door and turned the lock. It took only a few steps to cross the room to my dresser. I nabbed a hair tie from a small mess of them on the tray on my dresser and slipped it around my wrist. Then I gathered the greasy tendrils of my ruby-red hair into a bun. I neglected washing it since the morning of Mr. Stevenson's funeral. Thank God for dry shampoo.

Just thinking about that shitty day made me want to go to bed, pull the blanket over my head and go to sleep.

Not only had Mr. Stevenson died, but that funeral

reception was God awful. I had been concerned for Charlie's well-being since the night he showed at the door in tears after his dad was shot. Marisol and I plied him with drinks and sent him home in an Uber because we didn't have a couch and I sure as hell didn't want him in my bedroom.

How he knew where I lived, I'll never know. Over the duration of our relationship, he never came over or had spoken to me that much.

Seeing how we looked after him, only for him to treat me like trash at the reception, sent me down for the count. It was a betrayal, plain and simple and every time it came to mind, I felt rage and despair in equal measure. Any positive feelings I had left towards Charlie, vanished from the moment he basically told me to shove off in front of a crowd of people.

Why this kind of stuff happened to me, I never understood. It was like I wore a sign over my head that said it was okay to treat me like shit.

Luckily, I'll be on vacation next week, which was a relief because I could barely pull myself out of bed. One strategy that I implemented was turning up the volume on the alarm clock real high and placing it across the room so that I had to crawl out of bed to shut it off. Mom taught me to do that during my high school years when I was perpetually late making it to my first class, and the office phoned her while she was at work.

Sitting down in the office chair, I ripped open Marisol's envelope and pulled out a Christmas card. It had a silhouette of Santa and his reindeer flying in front of the moon over snowy rooftops. Inside the card had a twenty-five-dollar gift certificate to Hidden Féminin, a lingerie shop. She received the same thing from me because it was our standing gift exchange agreement.

I grabbed the green envelope from the letter basket with the familiar Oregon address, tore it open, and pulled out the card. The picture on the front had a Santa and Mr. Clause sitting on a beach, holding a glass and sipping from a straw. Inside the card was a fifty-dollar gift certificate to Wonder Grill Steaks. It read:

> *Merry Christmas, baby girl.*
> *Love,*
> *Mom.*

I pressed the card to my chest, then stood them up in the center of the dresser along with Marisol's card making them the only Christmas decoration in this room.

My phone rang with a new text notification. The time on the digital clock read 8:57 a.m. Which meant that it was 5:57 a.m. back home, and Mom wouldn't call that early, even though we hadn't spoken in a while.

I went to the side table by my bed, picked up my phone and Troy's name was on the notification. My stomach dropped.

After punching in my code, his message appeared on the screen.

**Troy Hanes:** Miss you. Miss those giant tits of yours. Call me.

Just like that, I felt like someone spat on me. I turned off the phone as unease slithered up my spine. Since the funeral, he sent similar texts. My plan was to ignore him and hope he lost interest. I had no desire to be the side chick to a married man, especially to one as mean as Troy.

In Charlie's case, we were seeing each other before he dated Carol Lynne, but he wanted to keep it a secret. Why? No clue. At first, I thought he was trying to role-play because we met in his office every Friday for a hookup, but he dismissed me after we were done. I hoped something more grew from it when we kept seeing each other, but it didn't. Eventually, he met Carol Lynne and ignored me altogether.

Another layer of weird was Troy. We had stopped speaking except at work when he asked for his messages in the morning. It was weird during the funeral reception when he followed me around even while his pregnant wife, Brianne, was there. It was both arrogant and creepy.

The thing was, Troy and I had a legitimate relationship where we lived together before he left me for the Park Avenue princess. They were expecting a baby, for Pete's sake. Why would he risk ruining that by contacting me?

*Men*. I'll never understand them.

Setting the phone down, I took the small pot from the coffee maker sitting on my dresser. I went out to the kitchen and filled it with some water from the sink, then came back to my room. Pouring it into the reservoir, I plugged the cord into the wall outlet, turned it on and started making coffee.

I pulled open the dresser drawer and took out a green mug that Mom had sent for my birthday last month. It had a white outline of a wolf surrounded by pine trees and the words *Davidson Sawmill* printed on the bottom. The sawmill was a company my mother inherited after Uncle Russ passed away unexpectedly from a heart attack about ten years ago.

Marisol and I stored food in mini-fridges in our

bedrooms because the kitchen didn't have one. That meant the space was super tight, and I had to find versatile ways of using storage. I only used the kitchen stove to cook or to heat something in the microwave.

After stirring the hazelnut creamer into my coffee, I returned it to the fridge. Holding my coffee cup, I grabbed the TV remote off the nightstand and flipped through a few channels of the overhead-mounted screen until it was filled with giant floats and college bands playing a merry ruckus of holiday music. Then, I settled on my bed, next to the stuffed lama Mom had sent for my birthday last year.

While I sipped on the creamy goodness, Marisol knocked and shouted from the other side of the closed door, "Chica, I'm leaving. You coming?"

"No thanks, I'll just stay in today," I raised my voice.

She acknowledged with a quick, "Okay," and left.

I got out of bed and set down the mug on the nightstand. Then I opened a cupboard mounted on the wall by the foot of my bed, and took a box of pancake mix and spray oil. I took the rest of the stuff from my mini-fridge beside my desk and headed to the kitchen. Finally, I fell into the practice of making my special occasions breakfast and eating it in the sparse living room which only had a dining room table and some chairs.

After making my second cup of coffee, I sat by the desk, chatting with strangers on social media when my phone rang. The screen read *Geraldine Davidson Calling*. My chest lifted as I swiped the green button.

"Merry Christmas, Mom," I greeted as soon as I put the phone to my ear.

Mom's deep, husky voice rasped, "Merry Christmas, baby girl." She quit smoking years ago, but it left a scar on her vocal cords. Call me crazy, but I loved its sound because it reminded me of a mamma bear.

"How are you? How's everybody back home?" I asked.

There was a pause, then she said, "Things are down because we had lost a chokerman last month, and everything was in chaos since Jax needed time off to deal with his death. That left Craig as my only feller."

*Lost* meant that someone died. The choker guy hung around on the ground while the fellers chopped down the tree. So the chokerman she was talking about was probably crushed to death, and the Jax guy was the feller responsible—that was if I read between the lines correctly.

"Oh, sorry to hear that. When did it happen?" I asked.

"Early last month, so Thanksgiving was depressing," she answered.

People were dying left and right. What was going on in the world? Did we enter some kind of shitty twilight zone?

After no response came from me, she prompted, "Hello? You there?"

"Yeah, sorry. Mr. Stevenson died last month, so I'm still reeling from that. Too many deaths," I said in the familiar sad tone that had become my regular way of speaking lately.

"Your boss? You're kidding. How come? Heart attack?" she asked.

"No, a home intruder shot him at his son's girl-friend's house."

Mom's inhale was sharp. "Amberly, I swear, that place is more of a wild west than anything we have here. I wish you'd give some thought about moving back."

I took in my cramped, shoebox-sized room. You could rent an entire house back home with the same money it took to rent an apartment here.

"I'll think about it, Mom. It's just that I don't want to leave things as chaotic as they are at work and run off. I'm staying out of respect for Mr. Stevenson. It won't take too long. Just until they get back on their feet."

Pain burned my throat, but I continued, "Besides, if I moved, where would I stay? I love you, but I don't want to live on your couch. And you just converted my old bedroom into your painting studio."

"I could move all my stuff out," she said with hope in her voice. "I can move the cot out of the garage into your room and we could get a dresser—"

"Then I'll be exchanging my life here for the same one there."

Mom said, "Well—"

I could almost hear the cogs in her brain turning.

"How about I help you find a place to live? An apartment all your own. It would be much safer than living in New York, and you won't have to hide in your bedroom all the time. And of course, you will always have a job at the sawmill."

I took in my jam-packed bedroom. There was no space to move around because I stuffed everything needed to occupy an entire apartment into a small bedroom. This apartment didn't even have a TV in the living room. We paid for our own cable service that was hooked up in our bedrooms. How awesome would it be if I could hang out in the living room at night?

"I'd like that. I'll give it serious thought," I said.

"Okay, baby girl," she said with a smile in her voice. That was the first time she really made headway in convincing me to move back home. It's not like I would ever run into *him*. He avoided me like I was the plague, and if we saw each other, he'd probably pretend to not notice me. That's the way he wanted it.

I tipped back my mug and swallowed the dregs of coffee to soothe my tight throat, then asked, "What else is going on? What kind of stuff have you been painting?"

"Mt. Hood. I'm concentrating on learning how to paint mountains before tackling flowers," she said.

"Sounds like a good plan. You know which show you should watch?"

"Don't say it! Everyone says it!" she said, making me crack up.

We spoke for a little while longer, then hung up. My heart weighed less than it had in weeks. But sad, too because I missed home because I'd probably be over at her house if I was there.

Since things didn't turn out how I'd hoped, maybe I should just move back. It wasn't like I gained anything by living here.

My phone buzzed with a text notification.


**Troy Hanes:** I called you and got a busy signal. Who were you talking to?

**Troy Hanes:** You move on fast, don't you?

**Troy Hanes:** From me to Charlie.

**Troy Hanes:** Will you ping pong back to me again?

**Troy Hanes:** Or are you sucking someone else's dick?

What. The. Actual. Fuck!

**Amberly Davidson:** What the fuck is your problem, man? Go back to your pregnant wife. Be a man, look after her and leave me alone!
**Troy Hanes:** :-)

God, he was getting creepier. Should I report this? But to who? My boss was now Charlie, Troy's brother-in-law, and at the moment, he was grieving. He wouldn't be able to help.

I tried to ignore the message and the creeped-out feeling for the rest of the day. The one good thing was that I was on vacation for the rest of the week, so I didn't have to decide now. Maybe things will cool down after the holidays.

Looking back on how Troy nearly killed me later that week, I should have listened to my mother and left immediately.

# AFTERWORD

Communes in the United States of America are a part of the Federation of Egalitarian Communities. The FEC started PEACH which is health insurance for the entire community and not specific individuals.

My take on this community is completely fictitious to serve the novel, and not based on the realities of intentional communities. For more information, please visit the Federation of Egalitarian Communities.

*Timberwolf*

*Ms. Judged*

www.ingramcontent.com/pod-product-compliance
Lightning Source LLC
Chambersburg PA
CBHW061308190726
48288CB00002B/404